LADIES

LADIES

RETOLD STORIES OF GODDESSES AND HEROINES

Doris Vallejo

Illustrations by
Boris Vallejo

A ROC BOOK

For my friends:
Chris Ganger, Rowena Morrill and George Smith,
each a lantern bearer in the darkness.
It is to them that these writings are dedicated.

ROC
Published by the Penguin Group
Penguin Books USA Inc., 375 Hudson Street,
New York, New York 10014, U.S.A.
Penguin Books Ltd, 27 Wrights Lane,
London W8 5TZ, England
Penguin Books Australia Ltd, Ringwood,
Victoria, Australia
Penguin Books Canada Ltd, 10 Alcorn Avenue,
Toronto, Ontario, Canada M4V 3B2
Penguin Books (N.Z.) Ltd, 182–190 Wairau Road,
Auckland 10, New Zealand

Penguin Books Ltd, Registered Offices:
Harmondsworth, Middlesex, England

First published by Roc, an imprint of New American Library,
a division of Penguin Books USA Inc.

First Printing, November, 1992
10 9 8 7 6 5 4 3 2

Text copyright © Doris Vallejo, 1992
Illustrations copyright © Boris Vallejo, 1992
All rights reserved.

 REGISTERED TRADEMARK—MARCA REGISTRADA

Library of Congress Cataloging in Publication Data:
Vallejo, Doris.
    Ladies : retold stories of goddesses and heroines / Doris Vallejo : illustrations by Boris Vallejo
        p.   cm.
    ISBN 0-451-45207-0 (hc.)
    ISBN 0-451-45107-4 (pbk.)
    1. Fantastic fiction, American. 2. Goddesses—Fiction. 3. Heroines—Fiction.
4. Women—Fiction. I. Vallejo, Boris. II. Title.
PS3572.A413L34   1992
813'.54—dc20   92–4482
                                                                      CIP

Printed in the United States of America
Set in Walbaum
Designed by Leonard Telesca

CONTENTS

PERSEPHONE

"DON'T PICK THE NARCISSUS . . ." MY MOTHER SAID. HER LILTING voice still echoes, even years later. When sunbeams danced in her hair she looked as golden as an angel. I loved her when she was golden. But I *wanted* those cloud-white flowers with their laughing purple eyes. Why shouldn't I have them—white butterfly dreams in a dream-strewn meadow? Why shouldn't I take them home with me? What harm was there?

My mother, who is abundantly kind and generous and wise, can be ruthless when she is opposed. She can retreat behind what ceases to be a face and becomes a wax-yellow death mask. She has withered leaves with her condemning gaze. I learned to circumvent her anger with hugs and kisses and seeming agreements.

But I wanted the narcissus more than I feared her condemnation. Who would not have risked such an obscure danger to gather them quickly, quickly before they faded; before they rolled up their shining faces and retreated, green-leaved, behind the camouflage of waving grass?

"Don't pick the narcissus," she said, in a cold, admonishing voice—as if I had already committed the sin and failed her irredeemably.

My beautiful mother.

I loved her intensely, with all the unquestioning adoration of a seedling for the sun. My heart first quickened in her womb, and I saw my first, glorious, vanishing rainbow through her eyes. She taught me what wishes were for, and how to keep them fresh and green so that every day was sweetened by the promise of their blooming. I had never doubted her, never questioned her judgment, as if to do so would be a betrayal. Yet this sinister warning incited my stubbornness. Even while I pretended agreement, a small angry thing hammered away inside me. Had it been there from the beginning, this anonymous rebel? Had it been dozing on and off in the secret darkness, content until then to flutter only feebly with life? Or had it been keeping that angry score for years which the weak tote up against the strong?

By what right did she forbid me those flowers? Narcissus, who once kindled heartbroken longings in foolish nymphs, was only a name, a sad legend, no longer real. He and his fate had nothing to do with me. Therefore—she had no right. Was it knowledge of her impotence that put the coldness in her voice?

I *wanted* those flowers. I wanted to tear them from their roots, as many as I could hold—to crush them into the circle of my arms, to take them with me.

"Don't pick the narcissus. . . ." Her teasing, ambiguous voice bespoke her displeasure and at the same time dared me to disobey. She told me how willful she had been as a child. Forbidden to befriend wild animals, boars, wolves, hyenas, and the like, she had done so anyway. In return they

brought her the mangled, often unrecognizable remains of their prey and left these dreadful offerings to putrefy among the roses and the lilies. She related these stories with a certain pride: *This is how I was. I was right to be so. I have always been right.*

I listened obediently and did fear the flowers she warned me against (pure white enigmatic faces concealing what treacherous secrets?), as if I already knew that the joy of possessing them might be terrible. And suddenly I hated her, though I denied that flash of hate even as it blazed; denied that shock, that first fierce rift between us, that awareness—growing hourly keener—that something had torn itself loose.

She refused to hear my cry for help when you brought me all the terrible way down here. Of course, by then it was really too late. What could she have done to stop you, to halt your lathered horses, your hurtling chariot? But the whole long time I have been down here among the dead, she has gone about lamenting her loss. *Her loss.* She assumed the guise of an ancient hag and let the resplendent Earth dry and wither. She mourned, and let her grief spread like a contagion. "If you had heeded me, none of this would have happened," she seemed to say. I found it a cruelly skewed accusation.

It has taken me until now to realize she never meant me any harm. It was not even me she was thinking of. She was absorbed by her loss—precisely that loss which she wanted to prevent.

I had always been like her shadow. I shouldn't blame her for seeking to constrain me. Consider the anarchy that would arise if we were all to have remiss attitudes toward our shadows. Animal shadows would one day be attaching themselves to men. Mice might scamper around trailed by bird shadows, children by the shadows of mountain lions, salamanders by elephant shadows, and so on. Some shadows would, naturally, fail to attach themselves anywhere. They would go roaming loose across rivers, through forests, in and about cities—getting lost, traipsing into the paths of horses and chariots, causing confusion, committing the irksome thefts blamed on dogs or the hapless spirits of departed relatives. This chaos surely ought to be avoided. Of course, there is another aspect of the matter to be considered: the woeful dependency of shadows.

I was still very little that day my mother and I lay side by side gazing into a pond reputedly inhabited by silver-finned naiads. (It may have been in this very pond that Narcissus drowned, trying to capture the flash and shimmer of his own beguiling image.) The glassy surface showed us two musing faces that but for the difference in age would have been identical. I saw my present and my future. I saw what I could become. And—I agreed to it. I had no inkling there might be another me that would not agree.

It has taken me until now to realize how this other me lay sealed off, entombed as in a coffin. Not really alive, it resembled those unborn wraiths wandering here along the shores of the Lethe: all those hollow angels, emptied of the memories and dreams that distinguished them from each other once. But the other me did have memories: a father on Mount Olympus who was so tall he dwarfed all by comparison. I believe he scarcely saw me when he looked down. My height, measured against his, was insignificant. (I had not yet learned the folly of measuring my height against his.)

Ah, yes, he must have known I was his daughter. But I was too close to the ground above which he towered for him to see how anxiously I craned my neck back to glimpse his face; how I strained to understand what he told me. "There are no more giants . . ." he said, and I nodded, though I was thoroughly perplexed. How could there be no more giants if he was a giant; his great size, his flowing black beard, the murderous thunderbolts he hurled so clearly denoting him as nothing less? I dared not reveal my ignorance. Only now do I understand. He was speaking of the Titans, whom he'd banished here to Tartarus. They had dared to hurl make-believe thunderbolts in an effort to appear as powerful as he. I wonder how many mortals were deceived by the glimmer and rumble of the puny torches they flung. And I wonder how, governed by such a tyrannical god, anyone ever dared anything at all.

There were other memories too, memories of what seemed like such wrenching losses. I discovered a sleeping fox in a bed of dry leaves. The leaves, crackling like unintelli-

gible voices under my feet, accentuated the fox's stillness. I feared that unnatural stillness. Yet I knelt down to see if, after all, the lovely orange fur did not embrace some sound—which it did: the sound of ants and maggots feeding.

There were memories of faces and the stories belonging to those faces.

There was the memory of a shy, graceful doe I wished to befriend and how wanting this friendship with all my heart failed to win it. How tears failed to win it. How anger failed to win it also. I could watch that doe from a distance for hours, but the slightest move towards her would send her into flight. In her bounding retreat she would appear to hang motionless in the air for whole moments—so teasingly mine, and so elusive.

Sometimes I think all the pictures indelibly stamped on the dark clay of memory were sly whisperings of your approach. I think that I was waiting for you, that some part of me was longing for you even before I knew you, that this body in which I lay dormant did prepare for loving you early on—with the mother it loved, with the father it was awed by, with every friend it embraced, every secret it shared with another, every joy it lost and found again.

You planted the path of white flowers across the meadow, though it hardly surprises me that you deny it. You knew their scent to be captivating, their beauty compelling. You knew how I would want them, how they would lead me to where you lay in wait. Your trap was so cleverly laid. Would it tarnish your victory if I told you I saw you hiding in the mists and in the dark bowers of trees? It was your infatuated vigil that made me bold. You thought I was inviting the sun's kisses when I stretched my naked arms toward its light and warmth. Yet it was you alone I thus immodestly invited.

I never expected you to lurch from the shadows and carry me off against my frightened, struggling will. I thought you would woo me more courteously. I dreamed you would charm me with stories, with music, with all the magic increments of love. Had our roles been reversed, had I your powers to enchant, I would have planted longing in your heart and nurtured it as shrewdly as ever my accomplished mother tended her gardens. I would have filled your dreams with me: my face, my scent, my touch, my cheek laid against yours, my breath so mingled with your own you could not help drawing it in throughout the rise and fall of sleep. Only then, when the longing had begun to flower, would I have made more urgent and more intimate demands.

But I am not you and neither think, feel, fight, conquer, or surrender as you do. Nor are you in any cell of your body like me. Thus it happens, I believe, that in appraising each other through blinkered eyes, we see mainly ourselves.

You came to me like an enemy. Can you perhaps imagine, my love, that a woman exists in my outraged soul who would have willingly given what you so crudely took? Yes, you tell me regretfully, now you know. And in the same breath you protest your blamelessness. You accuse me of damning you for illusory crimes, for wrongs that exist predominantly in my head—whence I refuse to expel them. Thus you moor the guilt neatly to my refusal. How human of you, my brute god of the shadows, to shift it to me.

You have one valid complaint. I've no wish to forgive you. Your "crimes" are the terror my dreaming self harshly awoke to—just as they are the weapons you put in my hands. Why should I relinquish my sorrow, my reticence, my averted gaze? They are far more virulent than any poison dropped in a goblet of wine, any sword raised against you, any arrow directed at your heart.

I lay beneath you and steeled myself as toward any plunderer, though hardly through fear of pain. My arms were thrown defenselessly wide, as were my legs. My eyes were closed over the fantasy that we were floating on ocean waves. I waited for your anchor to strike bottom. I listened to the song of your breathing above me. I abandoned myself to the sway and tilt of our rocking. But I was sand your hands kneaded, and I flowed away between your fingers. You seemed not to notice how less and less was left of me: only mouth and thighs and the place between my thighs, and finally nothing. This nothing gathered beside us and watched.

I lay beneath your kisses and my half-remembered body grew heavy with you. It loved you in secret: loved the feel

of your hands, your mouth, in secret; loved the naked places of your face out of which secret tears spilled and splashed into my eyes.

Who are you, my love, that, loving you, I seek to wound you? That, wounding you, I wound myself? Your gifts tell me something about you. You gave me a kingdom. You gave me a throne any lesser woman would shrink to sit upon. With keenest insight into the crueler part of my nature, you gave me the dread Furies as handmaidens. Desiring me, you invoked the goddess in me. Taking me prisoner, you invoked the demon.

Throughout the years I longed for you; not knowing who you were, I created my own portraits of you. You became the man who heard even that which I failed to say and saw even that which I failed to show. I cast you in the image of perfect counterpart only to be staggered by your moods, your wants, your kindnesses, your savageries—so strangely separate from my own.

You love me—so you repeatedly say.

Yet you turned your back and left me to explore this haunted kingdom by myself; to discover by myself how this barbarous land is unlike any place on Earth. You left me to wander unguided among the clamoring spirits, to find my way alone through the murk and confusion. You left me to ponder the relish with which I ate the pomegranate seeds you brought to me even as I suspected the danger therein. (*Suspected?* Ah, I did more than suspect—I knew I was sealing my fate. I knew I would not be allowed to return to Earth once I ate them. I knew!) We do disguise the traps we set for one other with such fanciful truths. Afterwards it was easy to damn you for those pomegranate seeds; to hate you for your trickery and your treachery.

I never imagined how the twilight here would shine through and through us, making us seem transparent as ghosts.

You left me to sit in that underground room with my futile rage and my grief. It wasn't long before I became aware of their poison blocking my heart, constricting my throat, welling up in my eyes. I wanted to smash, to destroy whatever I could lay my hands on: tapestries, chairs, bedclothes,

candelabra—reduce everything to rubble and to rags. Most of all I wanted to destroy you, to batter your flesh into pulp with my fists, to hear the crack of your bones. Would you have reminded me then of my beauty, my easy laughter, my songs; of all that charmed you about me?

What can we truly know of another's pain when we cannot see with another's eyes or feel with another's heart? You said: "I wake up and the thought that I deserve your hatred is the first thing in my head. You can't imagine how it saddens me, how it sickens me."

I understood the words only. There was too much silence *between* word and word for me to understand the rest.

You love me and yet you turned your back. So I decided to leave that room with its suffocating air. I had been sitting there in my white gown (like a bride dreading her wedding night) too long. Though no bolt slid in the door before you entered or after you left, I fully expected the door to be barred. I prowled back and forth in front of it. The futility of struggling to open it was monstrously real. I stopped and listened. I waited. I took up the prowl again until, in irritation at my own cowardice, I flung myself against the door and it swung open without resistance. I expected the guards stationed outside to stop me and was surprised to find only empty armor outside. Only robes draping nothingness. Only hoods framing darkness where faces might have watched.

I left the castle unaccosted. It felt good just to be walking. It felt, at first, like freedom. The physical effort made me almost happy before I became aware of the brutishness of this landscape. A scarecrow was pinned against the lifeless horizon of a barren stone mountain. Further on I came to a sulphurous steam that hissed out of a chasm. Human and reptile shapes writhed in that steam. Sometimes a screaming mouth or a reaching hand were visible; sometimes only a claw or a scaly section of coil.

The path I followed widened. I saw a demon flaying a group of the damned with a burning sword. One of the damned had torn himself open and was wrenching at his intestines. At least the demon left this one alone. Dreadful as his suicide's task was, I thought, he could rest from it when he chose; he could lean panting against the rock for a while and resume in his own time.

I came to a place where a forest once grew. Now stunted tree trunks with dry, broken branches jutted from the cracked ground. On my approach, those dead relics began to quake. They howled. They caught at my hair. They whipped at my face; they spewed their moldy dust in my mouth. In despair, I begged them to stop. Sores opened in the petrified bark. I pleaded with them to stop. Puslike sap vomited forth. With the strength of despair I commanded them to stop and the sores healed up. I commanded them to be silent and they grew silent. Once again they were inanimate sticks of dry wood.

Thus I realized it was time I cease mourning the girl I once was. It was time to let go of her, of how she once danced, of how innocently she once thought all things were possible. It was time to pick up my scepter and don my crown. This land of dark horizons does have its own bleak beauty. Orpheus found his lost Eurydice here. Here Tantalus, ever reaching for the receding fruit, finds in his very efforts the essence of hope.

I wandered near the banks of the Lethe, the river of forgetfulness. Hundreds of ghosts wandered alongside me. I neither acknowledged them nor troubled to avoid them. Either they floated out of my path or I passed right through them. When that happened, I could hear their garbled memories fading as the river water they had drunk took effect. There were so many of them, so many drifting, mumbling wraiths who had suffered an excess of living and dying, and who had accepted fiery lashes across their backs in an ecstasy of atonement. Now they were insubstantial as dust. I could make them vanish by closing my eyes.

A lady with white hair and diaphanous robes drifted into my path. Her nose was worn down to a tiny mound, and her mouth was a round hole from which faint breezes blew. I felt those breezes warm and putrid against my cheeks as I started to pass through her. Even as I recoiled, I recognized the link between us: the half-formed cry of the thirsting spirit forever drawn to mirages. I made her vanish, but others fluttered about me, signaled to me, called to me in their soft voices. The noisy dirge of their agonies and regrets sang insistently in my ears.

I could, I knew, drink my own forgetfulness from the Lethe. I knelt, though only to test its waters, to feel something of what those dead souls had felt. My hands shook as I cupped the icy water in them. It was colder than anything I had ever known, and for the first time I clearly understood how it could sap the warmer memories of life. I imagined plunging my face into the water. I imagined having my face grow indistinct. I imagined avenging myself on you by expunging all that is you from my mind: your face, your voice, your touch—all gone. I could have presented you with a bride emptied of even the most elemental of memories: the sound of rain, the sparkle of dew, the warm, fleeting beat of pleasure—all erased. Just imagining your shock at finding me thus made my hands tremble less.

But suddenly you were there beside me, kneeling beside me, putting your arms around me, your warm arms around my freezing ones. The water leaked back into the river from my hands. I watched it flow on. It glimmered with malice.

"What I did," you said, "I did out of the fear that you would not want me. And it's terrible to understand that— I who thought myself immune to fear."

Naturally I doubted you. Since when do gods fear?

You said, "I have been too influenced by the offerings always brought to me with averted eyes. I believed I was too dreadful to be looked upon. How should I have imagined that you might be anything but horrified at my approach?"

I reminded you that you are also called Pluto, the Giver of Wealth, and that this epithet might have been equally instructive. You might have brought me a cornucopia of fruits and flowers instead of fright and dismay.

"I wish you knew how much I do love you," you said.

Love, I answered, is a worn-out word used to flatter, to disarm, and to salve sundry ills. You think your claim of love should be sufficient to please me? I suggest it has always been yourself you loved best, your pleasure you sought first. You gave generously enough, but only what *you* wanted to give. How often did your gifts include what I wanted to have? How often did you ask what that might be?

"What do you want to have?" you asked, so openly chagrined I longed to comfort you with a passion that would no doubt have surprised you.

"Don't pick the narcissus . . ." How inextinguishably that warning resounds through my being! I believe it comes from before the time I was born. It transcends all subsequent experience. Else why should I not dwell on your gentleness, your concern, your many kindnesses toward me rather than cling to your single great offense, use it to shield myself from you?

You sought me out, chose me, loved me while I was only in love with shadows, while I was still judging the shape and worth of all things by their shadows. Were I to leave you in search of another man, more handsome, more powerful, more loving than you, I know in advance, I would not find him.

"I will make you happy," you tell me daily in the face of my resolute anger. What is such brave determination—the rarest gift or the greatest folly?

Oh, how I want to hold your face between my hands and kiss it, *kiss it!* I want to tell you what I've discovered: that the happiness of innocence I lost and mourned is shallow and trivial; that deeper joy must be forged out of groping and confusion, out of lying in the arms of indifferent lovers and knowing the emptiness of indifferent love; out of glimpsing a star-perfect moment in dreams and having it vanish on wakening; out of the quest to retrieve it. It must be forged out of endless puerile days spent wanting the wrong thing—or wanting nothing because all things, cursed with a most perverse Midas touch, turned to dust in one's hands. Out of hurting one's beloved and growing to understand that this might have happened because something was expected of us that we did not have to give.

I have stood at the ocean's edge and felt the power of its thrust against the shore through the soles of my feet. Thus I learned how variable, how indistinct was the division between a sea and a land that flowed so rapturously into one another. I learned it was up to me to make the distinction.

I do want to tell you what I've discovered here so that I can never again disclaim it: that innocence is the price to be paid for all things worth having.

Instead of saying anything, I gaze helplessly at you and am silent.

This, though, is where we are and how we came to be
here:

You called me yours; my body yours. Who gave you that
right? There I was with all my expectations. This is love,
I thought. This is love. This. And all I felt were my garments
being stripped from me like layers of skin. You tore them
in your haste, which I might still have found arousing had
you not been oblivious to my tears. As though tears endan-
gered you, you pretended that I did not cry or bleed or seek
to cover my nakedness.

Afterwards I let the Furies bathe me, perfume me, powder
me, paint a glistening red mouth on my face, outline my
eyes in funereal black. I dressed slowly in the silk gown you
gave me. I sat on the rumpled bed (avoiding the moist spot
on the covers) and leaned back against the large pillows.

Afterwards you turned from me with your failure, your
outrage, your bewilderment, your sense that I had cheated
you: I had smiled at you but not with joy, anticipated you but
not with eagerness, embraced you but not with passion.
My lips had pressed against yours too lightly for the kiss to
be construed as anything but dismissal.

"Do you ever consider how it is for me?" you asked. "What
it means for a warrior to be stripped of an armor he has
worn most of his life?"

"Yes," I said. "Of course I consider it. Daily. Hourly even.
But I can't *feel* it as I felt my own nakedness." I could tell
you thought it my failing not to be able to feel your ache.
Perhaps it is. And I wonder—isn't it time we grew beyond
our helplessness, we who have lost and gained so much at
each other's hands? Can't we learn some way to clasp each
other closer, to reach for the fragile, almost illusionary heart
within the heart, to hear its voices, to trace its moving,
changing shapes? To trace also the more tangible curves of
brow, cheeks, lips, chest, belly, arms, legs, and understand
that here, within this finite casing, is all the mystery, all the
splendor and anguish and strength, all the glances, words, tilts
of the head, all the perfumes, textures, gestures—all, in short,
that combines to become you whom I love?

There are whole hours when I imagine we can track down
the real failings and begin to mend them. But when I set

my list of things to do in order, I realize there is next to nothing I have not already tried, in one way or another.

Who are you but a man with secrets and surprises, a stranger whose delights and despairs are bound up with mine? Sometimes, when you reach out and stroke my hair or press your warm, strong face against my breasts, you become, as if by magic, as known to me as my own soul. Sometimes we are able to help each other. But can we, for that, begin to understand all the misunderstandings?

Here, in this dark uncanny world, I remember the sunny Earth as one might remember a dream. I long for it, as one longs for music, in a world of silence. Because I ate six of your pomegranate seeds, I am doomed to spend six months of the year here. I blame you for that. I despise you for it. Yet once I am back on the Earth again, surrounded by the comforting and the familiar, it is your absence that gnaws at me like a ravenous bird. Then the lack of you expands in me like a void, and the knowledge that you are here, that you love me, that you eagerly await me, is achingly precious.

Thus my joys are tainted with sadness in the spring when I leave you always to return. And my sadness is mingled with joy in the autumn when I return—always and ever to leave you.

Since I began my travels from the netherworld to this world of the living and back again, I have heard much that is curious about us: about the loves we discard, the fears we cling to, and the fables we invent to disguise or reveal them. At home on Earth, I have learned to call the underworld home. This bounded land has paradoxically broad horizons. Where else but here would poor Medusa's shade (cradling her severed head in folded arms) have stopped with me? And to whom else would that horror-haloed pate, its dry eyes ringed with crusted tears, have told her stories . . . ?

GORGON

EVEN AFTER IT HAPPENED AND SHE WAS NO LONGER BEAUTIFUL, she seldom lacked for lovers. True, she courted them with a resolve that approached madness. But they did love her. They never failed to tell her they loved her. Their avowals were her opiate, filling her with a warm, glorious peace and leaving her with an ever more desperate need.

From the day of her birth, she believed she was a monster. Not that this judgment had been formally passed. It was in people's eyes, however. It was behind their smiles and in the turn of their backs. It trailed her like a foul scent. She

could ignore it for days, for weeks; but it rose wolfishly around her whenever she was off guard. Trying to wash it off was useless. She rubbed palm oil on her face and breasts, marjoram on her eyebrows and into her hair, thyme on her throat and knees, mint on her arms, myrrh on her legs and feet. Still, throughout her youth and adolescence, it plagued her.

Once, on a stretch of empty beach, she lay on her back in the sand and, moving her arms up and down like wings, hollowed out the impression of an angel. Then she stood up to admire it. As her angel filled with the cold sea, that malignant odor rose plainly. Years later, alone in her den around which all the wild grasses had whitened to straw, she discovered that she enjoyed the smell. The scent of rot had an old familiar sweetness. Because she had hated it for years, being able to enjoy it struck her as a kind of victory. There was physical comfort in capitulation. The pungent caress of decay was palpably soothing.

Both of her sisters were immortal. It was cruel and unjust that she was not. Far from taking pity on her, they hated her for being (they thought) more beautiful than they were. They had brilliant smiles and alluring bodies; so what could they have been thinking of when they whispered together and laughed a secret laughter they would not let her share? It was only her hair that was lovelier than theirs— her long, swirling, shimmering hair that might have been sprinkled with dancing stars. One day it was gone, hideously changed into serpents.

From the mouth of her den she surveyed her statues, some of them age old, some of them newer and yet unchipped; all of them with their faces turned toward her, a congealed expression of love in their stone eyes. Their petrified bodies littered the mountainside and the surrounding land clear to the sea. The sight of them, which she had shunned at the start, now filled her with a great black surge of rapture. Yes, they had loved her.

Those inert lovers, still clutching their knives or swords, repeatedly came back to life in her dreams. An eye would blink. An outstretched hand would clamp into a fist. A foot would move. Within instants, they would be swarming up her mountain, the hum of their terrible ascent building. She would watch them come, their hate grown ferocious dur-

ing the years spent in limbo. Unable either to run or to turn them back into stone, she would helplessly murmur, "But I loved you."

They would tear her head from her neck and stuff it (its serpents still writhing, still spitting, still darting their red tongues at nothing, still snapping at nothing with their twin fangs) into a filthy leather pouch reeking of gore. She believed in the power of dreams to destroy and guarded herself against them by staying awake for days and nights at a time.

Because her perverse love for the stench of decay taught her the comfort of helplessness, she did not plan to defend herself should the dream become real. Instead, she would lie down at the mouth of her den, her hands with their slender fingers crossed on her breast, her eyes trustingly closed, unafraid.

She would let the nightmare burst blindingly over her.

Sometimes she was angry at her sisters for hating her. Sometimes she was sad. Both her anger and her sadness made tears trickle inward. They accumulated at the pit of her stomach and yearly grew weightier. She gave her sisters her prettiest dresses. She gave them her favorite jewels: silver bracelets, ornate combs for their hair, a string of emerald beads that heightened the green of her eyes. "What a beast she is," they whispered to each other, "giving us these cast-offs that are so gaudy, so ill fitting, so poorly cut and sewn they make us look like paupers! And for this she expects thanks." "I don't expect anything," she told them again and again. For years they turned a deaf ear on her. One day she decided to banish them from her world.

She collected strands of hair from their brushes. She collected their nail parings. She collected their discarded trinkets: an earring, a silver rose, a brooch with dulled pearls. She tied these things together in a bundle and flung them into the sea. "Now you are gone," she said. "Now you are dead." But they were not gone and they were not dead. They were immortal. She ceased speaking to them. She pretended not to see them. It went on for months. But they remained immortal, and the anguished desire for their affection burned ceaselessly in her.

BORIS ©91

She resumed seeing them and talking to them. She resumed giving them presents. She relied on this means of giving to transform indifference into love. The problem was that giving away so many of her treasures left her little to treasure. However, when she did not give her nice things away, they tended to get spoiled or lost.

She gave herself to countless men: to old men whose erections often slid softly from her before the end, to young men who pumped at her with the edgy, furious rhythm of rabbits and then went off to boast of their prowess. She gave herself to Poseidon, who, having impregnated her, vanished from her life. She gave herself to soldiers, to politicians, to peasants, to beggars. Once the serpents sprouted from her scalp, she destroyed all those to whom she gave herself by turning them to stone. In the end she sought to give herself to Perseus, who cut off her head.

Before Minerva changed her hair into serpents, she would brush it daily until it gleamed. "Do you think I am beautiful?" she would ask her admirers. "Did you think so from the first moment you saw me? Tell me what you thought, what you felt when you saw me. Tell me how beautiful I am." Eventually they stopped answering her, and she wondered if someone had banished her by flinging loose strands of her hair into the sea.

She first met Poseidon one day, as she was walking along the shore. She saw him in the distance astride the crest of a majestic breaker. He streaked toward her through the turbulent waves. His unexpected appearance and his seeming interest confirmed her earlier suspicions. Strands of her purloined hair must have been consigned to his sea. Obviously he had been charmed by the lovely hair. He swept close enough to the shore for her to see his luminous eyes, his strong mouth, the superb muscles swelling and sliding under his burnished skin. He swept close enough for her to feel a surge of victory. "Tell me how beautiful I am!" she cried. But he spun around in a burst of spray and was gone.

By the time they became lovers, she was no longer so certain of his fascination with her. "Tell me how much you love me," she demanded each time he came to see her. "Show me how much you love me. Give me proofs." She hungered for his reassurance and was disheartened by the silence of his body against hers. It was a measure of his callousness that he failed to understand her need. They made love (clearly nothing more than a performance) on the altar of Minerva's temple. "Do you find me beautiful?" she asked him. "You are as beautiful as a boa constrictor," he whinnied. Was it for this dalliance that cruel Minerva turned her hair into snakes? The idea to go there had been his, not hers. He had changed himself into a huge stallion, trumpeting his demand through redly flared nostrils. He had galloped ahead of her into the temple. What choice did she have but to follow him? He was unconcerned about the misery he caused her. But he left two pearls of light glimmering in her womb; two flecks of translucent light magically blossoming. Thus the act of love that joined them on Minerva's altar continued ever after to shackle her to him.

Throughout her life she dreamed about Perseus. The dream Perseus had set out on a worldwide quest to find her. Time and again he believed he had succeeded—now in the coquettish smiles and games of the naiads, then in the blaze of sun on the golden apples of the Hesperides. Lying on the hot sand in front of her den, aimlessly fondling herself, she awaited him. Even after her skin had coarsened and her body thickened, she was always slim and satin-smooth in the dream. She always had the sensuous curves of a mountain range. And he always found her. In the dream, she would know he was there without opening her eyes. He would stand at her feet, the sun flashing off his armor. There would be something menacing in his silent approval of her. Her trembling legs would begin to dissolve. She'd feel him bend over her, feel herself opening to him, feel herself suddenly transfixed, welded to him by the murdering stroke of his sword. It would be no more than a dream, but she'd feel it happening. And ... she would awaken to wonder ruefully with whom she was more truly linked, her discarded lovers or the lover of her dreams.

She wanted the immortality of her sisters, but she did not want their ennui, their pettiness, their eternal grievances. She wanted to sing bewitching songs like the Sirens, but she did not want the grim despair that gripped them when

Ulysses' sailors plugged their ears with wax and did not throw themselves overboard to swim to them. She wanted to be special, to stand apart from the gray mass of beings who passed anonymously through the world. She wanted to be loved above all others. She wanted to be the goddess of love. And she could not stop thinking that if anyone really knew her, her intrinsic worthlessness would ensure their contempt.

Did anyone care that her beauty had been wrongfully destroyed? Did anyone care that she grew daily more hated? Did anyone care how she suffered over this? Her entire happiness depended on the caring of others.

What she asked of her lovers was that they exact no commitments from her; that though they might fornicate with others, they desire only her; that they take her roughly, selfishly, cruelly even. They might bruise her flesh with their hands, but they must not ask anything of her beyond a passive surrender, a simple lending of her body to their pleasures. In return she offered to willingly bear whatever ignominy their love demanded.

One man, whose proclamations of love she believed most fervently, rarely made love to her. When he did, it was with an aloof, mechanical style. This made her cry. He then consoled her by saying that he wished to be with her forever; that he had no use for any life save one shared with her. He had the odious habit of farting loudly and frequently. One day she counted twenty farts. "Why do you have to do that?" she asked him. "Because otherwise I'll get a stomach ache," he said. "Why is it that you never farted when we first met?" she wanted to know. "Because I held it in," he said. So she asked him why, if he could live with a stomach ache when they first met, he couldn't continue to live with it subsequently. The day he left her, he struck her hard in the face. The taste and smell of blood in her nose were reminiscent of stone dust and dirt. Months later he sent her an odd gift (a gesture of reconciliation?), a rusted sword with the cutting side honed to a vicious edge.

Out of loneliness she took up with a simpleminded peasant. Since he was used to seeing snakes in the fields he farmed, he did not mind her writhing, hissing hair, though he took care not to be bitten. He planted a vegetable garden for her outside her cave. Because irrigation was a problem in that sandy ground; he hauled buckets of water there daily. But in making love, he kneaded her breasts as though they were the milk-swollen teats of a cow, her buttocks as though they were the fatted flanks of a pig, and he rode her with plowing, monotonous strokes just as if he were hoeing the earth. One day she said to him, "Do you see all the statues surrounding this place? They were all once flesh and pulsing blood. They were all my lovers." He looked mutely at the statues and held her hand. That night she dreamed she was buried beneath the garden he had planted. All the roots of the green growing things were tapped into her veins. Her body was shriveling and drying up under that garden. It was crumbling to sand. When she awoke, she tore up everything that was growing there and left it in a wilting heap. "I don't want to have vegetables!" she screamed at him. "They are repulsive with their scrawny stalks and their wormy leaves. Bring me one of your goats if you're so concerned what I eat! Bring me one of your precious geese! Bring me one of your calves!" Sadly he went off and returned with a plucked, eviscerated goose. She ate it raw, leaving him the wings and the bones.

One evening, directly after making love, he fell heavily asleep beside her. There he lay, a bulky ox, his arm leaden across her belly. She too must have fallen asleep, because it must have been a dream in which he was tearing the serpents from her head, plucking the claws from her fingers, eviscerating her with a long, curved blade in obvious preparation for eating. His face was distorted with crazy laughter. She struggled against him, struggled to free herself from his grasp. Her struggle and her wakening fused as if from opposite ends of the universe. She found herself, far from the den, in the shallow part of the river. She was drenched and shaking. Had he saved her from drowning? The tangle of serpents on her head was already awake, hissing, and alive with fright. They struck and struck at him, their long, thin tongues furling and unfurling, their fangs leaving dual pinpoint wounds that turned red at once. They struck him on the cheeks, in the eyes, on the neck, on the arms, and on the chest. When they struck him in the heart, he turned to stone.

She took up with a soldier. He was a mercenary who did

not much care whether he fought on the side of men or of the gods. He did not disguise this fluctuating loyalty. His virtue, he claimed, lay in his zeal for the truth. Upon her prompting, he told her that he loved her. As evidence he brought her the decapitated heads of foes. (She had confessed her fear of death to him, and these gruesome gifts, he explained, would inure her to such fears.) The truth, he told her, was that though she may once have been beautiful, now she was ugly. "I'd rather hear a pretty lie than an ugly truth," she said. He told her it was his imperviousness to beauty and ugliness, goodness and evil, life and death, that allowed him to love her. But he made love to her only in absolute darkness.

One day he lopped a serpent from her head. "Out of love," he insisted, spearing the twitching thing on the point of his sword. Other men had locks of their ladies' hair. He wanted this as a keepsake. Later she found it trampled flat in the sand not far from her cave. Flies were sucking at what had been its eyes. She tricked him into making love to her while her serpents were awake. They bit him and turned him to stone. "Now I can break you into tiny pieces," she said. She chipped away at his nose, his ears, his chin, gradually destroying his head altogether. Then she wept the many tears she had failed to wrest from him.

Near the end she often lay at the mouth of her cave and contemplated the surrounding assembly of statues. Unlike them, she was still able to cry, to bleed, to feel the precognitive fear of a lamb headed for slaughter. Her heart (already slowed like that of a dying beast) pumped on unwillingly under the sunless sky. She longed for the strength to dance naked and mad in that indifferent night. She longed to be empty, devoid of need and pain. She longed to be simpler, to be an animal, with an animal's baser sensibilities.

Near the beginning she loved to pretend that she was a wild mare. She imagined herself with a mare's vigor and swiftness and grace. She galloped along the moonlit shore at low tide, moon laughter singing and echoing around her, a warm wind tangling her splendid mane, her bare feet leaving hoof prints in the wet sand. Near the beginning she believed in happiness. She was buoyant with happiness.

Toward the end, her iniquitous quest for happiness had become an anchor, weighting her, mooring her to her violent fate.

She laughed easily. She could laugh for no reason at all. As a little child she laughed over certain sounds, certain shapes: the wind sighing in the treetops, the play of shadows and light on a wall, the face of the moon appearing and disappearing behind clouds. Later on she delighted in hearing and retelling amusing stories. On the retelling, however, they were invariably less amusing than when she first heard them. Still, she would laugh heartily and sometimes that was good enough to make her audience laugh too. The stories she told about herself usually inspired laughter, particularly when she portrayed herself as a fool.

After she grew accustomed to the snakes on her head, to their hissing, to their striking on their own volition, to their ferocious appetites upon wakening, she found her transformation from beauty to harridan rather a joke. At first she tried to hide the snakes under colored scarves. After some years she tired of this effort. "What difference does it make anyway?" she said to her sisters. "Men love me the way I am."

To her dream Perseus she said, "When I looked beautiful, I was ordinary and dull. Now that I am a monster, I am more unique."

As a child, she felt safest when she was ill. Those were the times she was absolved from chores and allowed to stay in bed. Also, her mother was tender then rather than critical. As she grew, she became increasingly aware of her body and its changes. She was extremely sensitive to heat, which depleted her physical strength, and to cold, which sapped her spiritual energy. Anger over real or imagined slights could be so fierce as to leave her breathless. As soon as she and Poseidon finished making love on Minerva's altar, he accused her of disinterest. When her protestations proved insufficient to convince him otherwise, she grabbed a chalice from the altar and smashed it against her head. Her blood flowed from the wound in thick rivulets. (Was it from these that the serpents sprang?) The sight of her blood-soaked hair stunned him into a kind of remorse.

Whenever she turned one of her lovers to stone, she asked his forgiveness. His silence, interpreted as a refusal, depressed her sorely. She would lie on her back in her den, gazing down at her motionless hands and legs and feet, thinking: This is how they will look when I'm dead, just like this. To avoid the inevitable, she would plead with her dream Perseus, inventing both her dialogue and his. Over and over she begged his forgiveness. Over and over he assured her that she was forgiven.

She fled from her fate as from devils. To escape it, she fell in love again and again. Each time, she feared that her new lover would eventually manifest his love with a reaping hook. All her life she struggled against this fear. She took pride in her courage in falling in love. Yet these flash-loves, all begun with hope, all ended with the knell of doom. Even so, she continued falling in love on the premise that somewhere along in time *the right one* would appear to free her from her fate, to make her beautiful again, to make her good. She yearned so to be good. Beneath the serpents, the coarse skin, the furious eyes; beneath the hatred, the anguish, the envy; beneath the cynic and the destroyer, there lay (like a butterfly in its chrysalis) a soft and trusting Medusa, an innocent and vulnerable Medusa, a very young and loving Medusa much in need of care and comfort.

Early on she was taught that truth was good and falsehoods were bad. This simplified the world and her position in it. "I can choose to be good or I can choose to be bad," she said. It was considered a profound philosophical observation for such a young child. She was called "bad" (although she had not chosen to be so) when she expressed a dislike for one of her mother's admirers. "Your wickedness is the reason you have no wings," her mother said. "Wicked people never learn to fly." "You're a liar," Medusa answered, for which her mother struck her across the mouth without warning.

People believed her sisters' lies. Their deceptions were generally rewarded. They stole some coins their mother had hidden in a clay pot and the theft was blamed on her. She felt this must be due to some theft she'd once committed and had forgotten about.

She discovered that her sisters were immortal because their father was immortal. Whether he was a god or a demon was never too clear. Her father, on the other hand, was merely one of the many men her mother referred to as their "uncles." The truth came to light one day when he was killed in a drunken fall from a horse. "Why didn't you tell me he was my father?" she asked her mother. "Why did you pretend he was just an uncle?" "I never pretended," her mother said so emphatically that she fully understood it must be her own perceptions that were at fault. When Minerva jealously destroyed her beauty, she was outraged at first. Later, when everyone seemed to consider Minerva's vengeance an apt punishment for unconscionable vanity, she was largely mollified.

At the outset of every affair, she dutifully warned her lovers that she would eventually turn them to stone. Thus she hoped to be absolved, beforehand, of any guilt in their destruction. Whenever she dreamed of Perseus beheading her, death was always painless. Murdering her seemed to confirm the depths of his love: not only had he braved great dangers to find her, he had excised all that was wrong and ugly from her.

When she and her sisters were little, they liked to play goddess. Insects, lizards, frogs, and the like became their subjects. They ruled these creatures capriciously, maiming and murdering them or else bringing them food and building them shelters out of grass and mud. Once they captured a chameleon and delighted in watching it change colors as it crawled across the sand, pebbles, bits of wood, grasses. Then her sisters began to torment it, tickling it with long reeds, snipping off the end of its tail, frustrating its attempts at escape. When she objected, they turned on her, calling her stupid and ugly, claiming she was not really a goddess and therefore had no say in its fate. Thus goaded, she slammed her fist down on the little creature, ending its magical color show forever. Far from being upset by this, her sisters laughed and said they didn't care.

I am like that chameleon, she thought, for she found herself changing in accordance with the company she was in. With some people she laughed and talked a lot. With others she was silent and solemn. There were those with whom she was tender and caring and still others who elicited her viciousness. No one of these moods reflected her real self any more than the others. Like the chameleon, she had no true color, only that borrowed from her surroundings.

As she got older she began to understand how illusions were created: different Medusas could be produced by a propitious selection of disclosures. To her lovers she told of her misadventures: how she had been taken advantage of, used, betrayed; how she had failed. To her sisters and to other women she boasted of her conquests and her successes. To her mother she continued to present herself as a child, always asking naive questions, always asking advice, always bringing her little please-love-me gifts: a bouquet of flowers, a scarf, sweets—things that she liked herself but for which her mother had no use.

All the illusory Medusas were real after a while. The angry and vengeful Medusa was real. The helpless Medusa was real. The mischievous Medusa was real. The mournful Medusa was real. There was no question of attributing the emergence of these various Medusas to the equinox or the phases of the moon, no chance of dispelling them, blowing them away like tumbleweeds across the sand. Fear and anger and madness went twittering through her veins like rabid bats. Murderous impulses were starkly real. It was her grief and guilt over the murders that was suspect. Just as her passion for loving and making love was—for all its dazzle—suspect. Her passion was far less substantial than the rainbow-hued scum slick of sweat on her flesh. All her generous acts, her kind words, her sweet kisses were suspect. Her ugliness was real.

She made pets of creatures not in general favored as pets: spiders, field mice, snakes, even rats. Two rats were in the habit of coming to her for scraps of food. Their dependence on her bound her to them. She played with them. Sometimes she dressed them up in her jewelry: wound her necklaces around their plump bodies, placed her bracelets on their heads like tiny crowns. She envied the companionship they gave each other. One day she saw a rat eating a baby bird and realized they would not starve without her. From that point she had no more interest in them. Subsequently she developed an aversion to rats. The sight of them, either dead or alive, revolted her. She was sunning herself on the patio of her mother's house when she looked up to see a large gray rat staring at her. It's going to bite me, she thought. Instead, it ran off as soon as she moved.

The first time she held a snake in her hands, she was surprised at the feel of it, which was not slimy and cold but dry and smooth. For a while she kept a collection of snakes in a box. They didn't need much care. Between their infrequent feedings they slept. People resisted her invitations to hold them or even look at them. This made her all the more insistent on showing them. After the snake period, she made a pet out of a black, furry spider. She caught flies for the spider, but, as far as she knew, it never ate them. Seemingly it preferred to catch its own victims. It bit her on the hand and the entire hand along with the forearm swelled up. When black moods descended on her for no apparent reason, she attributed them to the spider venom, which, she decided, had remained in her body.

Because she was often mocked as a child, she yearned for a child of her own that would only be admired. She believed that having a child would redeem her. Animals, suckling their young, seemed to transcend themselves. Nursing mothers looked saintly to her. When she was so plagued by premonitions of doom that she longed to be someone else, she took comfort in knowing that at least one day she would give birth to someone else, someone wonderful—a warrior perhaps, or a winged horse.

She found a baby bird that had fallen out of its nest. As she held it, the bird's naked wings fluttered in an affecting imitation of flight. She would have liked to nurse it back to health; but it died in her hand, its frail, bloated belly purple and round, as if with a rotting pregnancy. That night she dreamed about it. In the dream she and the bird were interchangeable. At times she was herself; at times she was the broken, flightless bird. In both cases the bloated belly was hers. As the dream ended, she gave birth to a black river of putrid blood. "You are afraid of dying," her sisters said loftily, their arrogance clearly based on their immunity to death. "You are like the fool frightened by his own shadow," they said. In fact she did find her own shadow distinctly frightening.

She enjoyed the singular odor of her menstrual blood; that smell from her womb, so distinctly hers. Later on, she cherished the two jewels glimmering in her womb: those starfish gently cradled in her ocean. Their hearts (as if with fright) throbbed so rapidly at first, she would fold her hands on her belly to soothe them. At times she could trace the outline of a tiny warrior beneath her taut skin. At times she could feel the head, the winged trunk, and the legs of a horse. She could feel its miniature hooves galloping madly under her heart.

Both her sisters had wings and could fly. When they were little they liked to taunt her by circling above her head and urging her to join them. She'd flap her arms wildly, determined to fly—which only emphasized the inequalities between them. Every evening before going to sleep she prayed that she would wake up with wings. Eventually she tired

of praying. Occasionally she dreamed that she could fly, that with sufficient concentration and will it was possible. The dreams were so real she always awoke believing it must truly be possible if only she grasped the secret.

Once Poseidon took her to his kingdom beneath the waves. There she could rise over the highest coral mountain just by turning her face toward its glistening peak. She could descend into the deepest blue-green valley by looking into its depths. "This is like a dream," she said to him. Breathing under water came effortlessly when she was with him.

When Icarus flew so close to the sun his wings melted and he fell to his death, she was both sorry and glad. She experienced the flight of this mortal as an affront and felt vindicated by its failure. Still, his brief victory was a kind of victory for her too. So it is possible, it is possible! she thought.

More than ever she became fascinated with creatures that flew. She studied them closely and discovered that the ability to fly was *not* linked to any virtue. Not only gods and birds flew. The hideous Furies flew. Bats flew. Certain dragons sprang into existence already equipped with great leathery wings. This made her question to what extent her vileness was at the root of her inability to fly and to what extent this shortcoming could be blamed on the conceits of the gods.

If I can't fly, at least I can leap, she decided. She leaped with ease over a beached crab on the sand. She drew two lines three feet apart in the sand and leaped over them. She drew the lines four feet apart and leaped over them too, but not as easily. She thought: *If I do this every day I will eventually be able to leap farther than anyone else, and that will be almost as good as flying.* Daily she practiced leaping over lines that were drawn ever farther apart. Eventually she was able to leap as far as a horse. One day she came upon a chasm worn into the earth by an ancient vanished river. The sight of the stony river bed far below rocked her with giddiness. Though the chasm was no broader than her broadest practice leap, she knew that clearing a space marked off in the sand was not the same thing as hurtling across an abyss. So she did not try. In later years it became difficult to believe she had ever attempted to fly with any real expectation of success. What is a dream, she thought, but an Achilles' heel, a place for a poisoned shaft to enter?

She could not remember being suckled at her mother's breasts, which, withered and sagging by the time the woman was thirty, looked as if any milk they might have given must have been watery and bitter. When her breasts grew plumply inviting, she was able to put her own nipples into her mouth and to suck at them. The sensation was pleasurable enough, but they gave no milk.

She wondered how satisfactory her sisters were as lovers. She imagined them in the act of love with various men. She imagined herself making love with them: the resilient softnesses of their buttocks, their breasts; the luxurious joy of being wrapped in their huge wings. She dared not suggest any of this to them and considered herself loathsome for thinking it. Still, she would caress her own body, noting its contours and textures, and pretend it was someone else she was touching.

The creature who fathered her sisters visited occasionally. Sometimes he appeared as a beam of light, sometimes as a Centaur, sometimes as a gryphon. As a rule he barely noticed her during these visits. However, it was as a gryphon that he flew through her window one night. She was awakened by the hard thump of his body alighting on her bed. Without much in the way of a greeting, he began to probe between her legs with his sharp talons. Until then she had not been aware that, aside from a means for elimination of wastes, there was anything of interest between her legs; therefore, his absorbed attention frightened even as it flattered her. When one of his talons pierced her skin, she cried out and shrank away from him, shudderingly protecting the injured place with her little hands. On his subsequent visits, the creature displayed his old indifference to her. Thus she believed that had she stifled her fear and succumbed to his hurtful caress, he would have loved her.

Once in a great while she was given a sweet. As long as it was sugary and real in her mouth she felt good. As soon as it was gone she felt lost again. The long periods of loss between sweet and sweet became unendurable. She began to steal sweets from their hiding places in the house and also

from the market. Her appetite for them always exceeded
the amount she could get. She recognized her greediness as
something shameful and wished she could be rid of it.
Since this was unlikely, she indulged it in secret. Sometimes
she fed until it seemed she would burst. Then she vomited.
Her stomach, abruptly delivered of its freight, contracted like
an empty womb. Once the serpents had sprouted from her
head she became less selective about what she ate. Anything
edible sufficed. There was no problem getting berries and
roots. She could yank them from the ground or tear them
from the bushes. It was another matter with live prey. She
had to approach it with stealth lest it turn to stone and become
inedible.

 Though in her last years she withdrew to a land perpetu-
ally inhabited by night, she loved the day. A seeming con-
tradiction; yet she was a creature of contradictions. What of
her single-minded yearning for Perseus, who awaited her
hand in hand with death? How did that need coexist with her
fear of dying? What of her simultaneous fondness and disgust for the serpents on her head? What of her sense of alien-
ation from all she needed and loved? She had reasons for
every paradox. She had a wealth of explanations. For instance,
about the serpents she said that the transformation from
beauty to grotesque, though regrettable, was a fine means of
sloughing off the chaff; of expediently weeding out all
those shallow men who could have embraced only the angel
in her and never the beast.

 When she awakened in her den and the darkness pressed
against her as it would in a grave, she always closed her
eyes tightly again, seeking the sanctuary of sleep. Sanctuary:
had it not been promised once? Had it not been guaranteed
when she was very young? As a reward for being good? How
much goodness was required? Days of it? Years? A lifetime?
A lifetime of goodness in exchange for one day of real peace?
Probably, she thought toward the end, even a lifetime of
goodness would be insufficient.

 When she was still beautiful, it used to take her nearly
two hours to prepare herself for the day: to perfume herself, to dress, to paint her face, to fix her hair, to eat—all that
in the hope of taking one tiny step closer to happiness. She spent
hours spinning thread for her loom, on which she planned to

weave fabulous tapestries for which she would be admired
and loved. But the tapestries, often begun, were never finished. The little flower gardens planted were never culti-
vated. The loves pursued were eventually abandoned. As a
monster she needed hardly any time to begin the day. She
stretched, yawned, rolled over slowly to ease the stiffening in
her joints, and listened for the bristle of wakening serpents. That was all the preparation needed for a day spent
stalking, hunting, and finally feeding on the stunned, still-
fluttering hearts of her prey. She had ceased to live like a
human being, although she continued to think of herself
as human. She continued to want and need and struggle
toward some vision of human joy. And she continued listening to her own fluttering heart cry for this man who would
soon still it.

So much of her strength went into preparing herself for
him: fattening herself up for him, accumulating sin upon
sin that his task might be easier. She made herself ugly for
him that in destroying her, he might emerge as beautiful.
She made herself feared to ensure that his victory be judged

courageous. She fashioned herself as a villainess (selflessly omitting no cruel refinement) that he might be cast as a hero.

And Perseus—who at long last did find her—looked only at her reflected image in the shield, never at her. He only pretended to see her. He only pretended to see that she loved all those she had turned to stone and that she greatly regretted all that had gone wrong. Perseus. How he made her pay for her dreams—her bungled dreams.

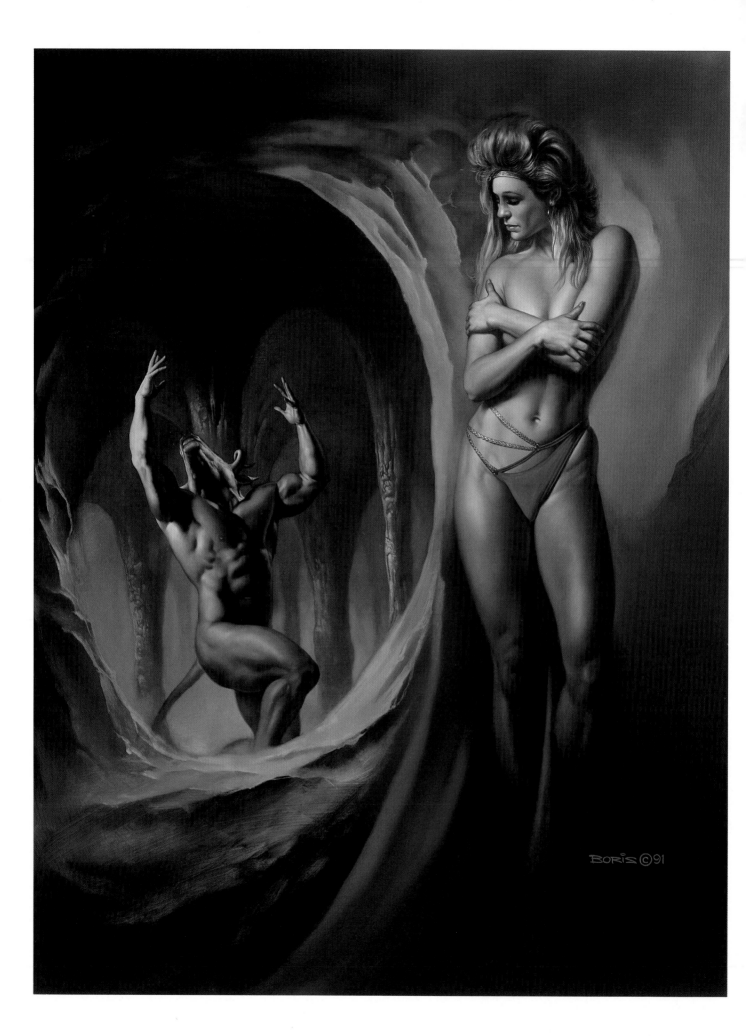

. . . *How* foreign the familiar can become! How alarming even the dawn can become, even opening your eyes can become when they seem to tell you nothing has changed and strangely, incomprehensibly, you know this is not so. Your own mirror image conspires with a suddenly baffling world to present a pleasant, clear-eyed face one day, a dull-skinned and malevolent face the next. Can Ariadne discover all the faces? Will she recognize them as her own? Does she believe recognition brings understanding? Does she believe in the courage to understand?

*A*RIADNE

THE MINOTAUR BELLOWED HIS ANGRY DESPAIR THE WHOLE NIGHT long. His tortured appeal echoed through tunnels that ever and again curved back on themselves. It reached her as an inhuman cry: "LET ME FREE! LET ME FREE!" Harsh, daunting, coldly alive, it penetrated the many walls between them to toll relentlessly in her ears. Pressing her hands hard over them only served to alter the sound, not to kill it.

She had been born with that onerous cry in her ears. This alone served to deafen her to it. She may have been fifteen or sixteen when a cry identical to the one from the Labyrinth first echoed from her own heart. Since the heart, a mindless muscle, could not physically produce a voice, she ignored it to begin with. Gradually, however, the world, which had always been sane and predictable, filled with disquieting omens. Nothing tangible changed. The routines of the day remained the same. Those who peopled her life—servants, courtiers, friends, teachers—carried on their affairs in customary fashion. Only she was different. Like an animal that can hear things inaudible to human ears, she became sensitive to a new scale of sounds: fear twisting through a high-pitched laugh, sly satisfaction at the core of remorse, anger cloaked in conciliatory words . . .

She had a clear view of the outside of the Labyrinth from her bedroom window. It was a remarkable fortress made of thousands of stones so smoothly fitted against one another, the might of an army could not have dislodged them. It had never been a secret that there was a creature imprisoned in its bowels. With the assurance born of naiveté, she relied on his sentence to be just. How could it be otherwise? The king had decreed it. She assumed the creature must be content in his prison. After all, seven youths and seven maidens were sacrificed to him yearly . . . as though he were a god. And, she half believed, perhaps he was. When she consciously heard his cries for the first time, they were oddly familiar. Speaking as they did of outrage, of terror, of loss, they evoked a poignant if abstract memory: as if with that sound, distant and alien griefs were transfused into her soul.

Ariadne: her dreamy gaze held the gentle timidity one might see in the liquid eyes of a fawn. Yet, on *hearing* the Minotaur's cry, she suddenly knew how it felt to tear the limbs from a struggling thing; she knew the taste of warm raw flesh; she knew the stench of despair: as if she had carried these things with her all along, like torn scraps of a picture slipped into a pocket—scraps of harmless colored papyrus that once pieced together presented a vivid and terrible scene.

The Minotaur was often mentioned in conversation. Yet nothing definitive was said about him. What was glossed over was provocative. What was explicitly stated was not. She asked what he looked like. "A bull's head and a man's

body," she was told. No one seemed to know how the head blended into the body. Did the bull portion end abruptly at a fur-ringed neck to leave a smooth-skinned body that was unmistakably human? Was this an athlete's body? Was it lithe? Graceful? Was it a grotesquerie stunted by its cramped and sunless domain? Or were the markings of its hybrid heritage commingled; the distinctions between man and beast blurred? The creature might have a bull's muzzle, a bull's horns, but also the high, intelligent forehead of a man. It might have a man's chest and shoulders, a man's arms and hands, but legs that tapered to cloven hoofs.

There was also the question (never clearly answered) about what the thing ate the whole long year between human offerings. Leaves? Berries? Insects? Rodents? Shanks of anonymous meat? And what did it do when it was not feeding or sleeping or howling? What were its wanderings like along the ever-intersecting, ever-horizonless passages? She listened in vain for a clue, a disclosing word to slip through the surface chatter. But even without it, she somehow knew . . .

The group of young Athenians slated for sacrifice to the Minotaur was a favorite subject for speculation at court. Could it be the proximity of doom that lent them their vibrant beauty? If, through some unlikely event, they should be freed, would they in consequence appear ordinary and drab? What a misfortune that would be—such charm, such loveliness corrupted! . . . Suppose, one day, one of them killed the monster instead of being killed by him. Was that possible? Was it even desirable? Wouldn't life without him be strangely terrifying? But it would never happen. No one, Ariadne thought, could possibly equal the beast in strength, in ferocity.

In theory the Minotaur could certainly be killed. He was mortal, after all. His mother was mortal. And his father . . . Yes, yes, there was the delightfully scandalous tale (told on the back stairs and only in whispers) of how Pasiphaë, the queen, had fallen in love with a bull—truly a splendid specimen, but a bull nonetheless.

Ariadne wondered about this unorthodox passion of her mother's. "Was it his golden fur?" she asked the absent woman. "Was it his great strength? Was it the seductive challenge of an inhuman mate?" Pasiphaë, who had been banished to the Labyrinth some time after her mongrel son, sent back no answer.

Slender Pasiphaë, with the flowing hair and gentle hands, drifted cloudlike through her daughter's memory. Pasiphaë: that insubstantial mother whose face could not be remembered and whose form could not be embraced. Pasiphaë was, even so, the one Ariadne most questioned. "Do you miss the sunlight, or is the darkness a comfort? Do you miss the sounds and scents of the outside world? Surely you must. And yet . . . ? What sort of life is it in that place where nothing can flourish save rats and spiders? Do you know a dependable way through the crisscrossing paths and wrong turns?"

No doubt the existence of the Minotaur was, to King Minos, a devastating reminder of his wife's strange dalliance. Small wonder that he relegated her son to what was, in effect, a dungeon. But why hadn't he simply killed the wretched thing? How could he bear the awful nightly howling? Ariadne was often on the verge of asking her father this question. She practiced asking. She worded and reworded it. In the end, fearing to hear his answer, she remained silent.

Minos was born into the conviction of his superiority, his unchallengeable rightness. His scheme of things was sacrosanct. His justice was simple. Theft was punished by amputation of the thief's hand; scandalmongering by excision of the tattler's tongue; insurrection by imprisonment; and cowardliness by death. He did not discuss or debate. He ruled.

On a certain gray afternoon, when the storm-auguring heavens constricted the world, Ariadne played a curious game. She pretended that the darkening room with its pillars and lounges was the Labyrinth. Somewhere, in a corner, in a doorway, under the wide bed or behind a bureau, the Minotaur crouched, watching.

If only she knew where. If only she could detect some outline in the shifting patterns of encroaching dark. Suddenly a curtain swayed and she saw him: an amorphous, swelling, growing slime that rose up toweringly above her. A scream, barely begun, congealed in her throat.

The breeze died and the curtain grew still. The Minotaur became two-dimensional and vanished into the silken folds. He was not, had not been, lurching at her. That had been a mistake, an illusion. She breathed with relief. Then, without warning, he reappeared, now coiled snakelike on the floor at her feet. One breath, one heartbeat would cause him to strike. Her mouth went suddenly dry. Her lungs, her heart were paralyzed. Death gazed from the creature's empty eye sockets. A burst of thunder exploded nearby with a bestial roar . . .

On a chill, stormy afternoon, when the growing dark threatened to obscure the world, Ariadne played a curious game. She pretended that she was the Minotaur, exiled to the terrifying loneliness of the Labyrinth. She shivered in her hiding spot among the folds of the curtain. She waited for the lightning flashes to illuminate the boundaries of her shrinking prison . . .

These might have been games to pass the sluggish hours, but they cast a lingering spell. They influenced her moods. They colored her waking and sleeping hours. The lament that rose from the Labyrinth continued to grieve as well as to comfort her. But with these games, the suggestion took root that it must one day be stilled.

Long beforehand she knew how it would be: the dagger smuggled into the Labyrinth under a cloak, the stalking, the waiting, the alert listening, the jolting moment of encounter, the attack, the dodging, the opponents locking on each other, the struggle, the first surprised grunt of pain, the blood, the terror, the frenzy, the exhilaration, the fatal final thrust. After that—a murderer's heart would beat in her breast always, always. . . . Long beforehand she dreamed of this death and was afraid.

"Why are you crying?" the king asked. He had come upon her in the rose arbor, where she sat weeping on a small stone bench. Because the whys and wherefores of her tears could not be reduced to explanations, she only shook her head. As she looked up at him, however, she became enchanted by the rich fabric of his cloak. Sunlight seemed to dance there in the gold threads. She wanted to touch them,

to feel the sparkling light on her hands. But he was not standing close enough for her to reach.

She saw that his well-tended beard, which had always been pure brown, was streaked with gray. The movement of overhead branches cast incessantly changing shadows on his face. These seemed, in their ebb and flow, to embody his sinister thoughts.

"What nonsense," he said, looking beyond her. "Either you are refusing to tell me the reason, or there is no reason and you're crying for nothing." After he left, it occurred to her that she was crying over the Minotaur, over her dual fear of and longing for his death.

It was more than a year later that she first heard of Theseus, the Athenian prince who had volunteered to fight the Minotaur. Did he actually hope to win? Quite likely he was mad. What else could such a grandiose display of patriotism be? These were times when madness wore faces of valor, of allegiance, even of wisdom. It was rumored that he was the son of Poseidon. More probably, he was just a strong swimmer. In either case—what did it matter?

All the talk about him set her imagination to working, however. The instant she saw him, she felt he would play an integral part in her life. She could help this man triumph over the Minotaur. Through him she could bring the dreaded and desired event to fruition. Should she give him the dagger she'd hidden away when the Minotaur's dirge first troubled her sleep? Was it wrong to weight fate in his favor? Or was it still more wrong to deny this urge? If only she knew which of the stories about him were really true.

When King Minos threw his ring into the sea, daring Theseus to retrieve it, the latter dove after it without hesitation. Either he believed the lofty talk about himself or he was not afraid of death. Once he disappeared beneath the rough waves, she half prayed he was gone for good. If he drowned, she need not think of him further. Her days might yet continue as before, and she could rout the troublesome murder plot that was hatching in her mind on its own volition. But if he emerged alive out of the blustering sea . . . ?

Like an animal that gnaws itself free of a trap and loses a leg in the process, one does not wrench oneself free of a constricting life without losing much that is precious. Still, it was impatience rather than fear that made her tremble as she gazed at the dark green water. She wanted to rush the seconds ahead, to eliminate the waiting, to know at once whether he would drown or reappear, the waves splashing silver from his head and the ring shining in his upraised hand.

He *will* drown, she decided. The water is too deep. Except through a miracle—indeed, the intervention of Poseidon— he will not find the ring. It was as good as lost the instant it left the king's hand. It is as good as buried under the uninterpretable ripples of the ocean floor. The more she thought about it, the more certain she became that her old life was safe. He had no chance of finding the ring and only the slimmest, swiftly diminishing chance of returning alive. The assembled Cretans were silent, as if his death had already been announced. Perhaps because of this she dared to imagine his return, dared to imagine him breaking from the green waves, rising effortlessly out of the deep sea, a smile on his bronzed and gleaming face. And as if by imagining it, she had caused it to be: *there he was . . .*

Theseus. He was not much taller than she, and not much older, though he had already slain a giant, beheaded the murderer Procrustes, and eluded a death the witch Medea had brewed for him. Theseus: her enemy or her salvation?

It might be true that Poseidon had guided him to the shores of Crete. But from the shore onward it was for her to guide him or to let him founder in the Labyrinth. That choice bound them to each other as surely as siblings are bound by blood and lovers by passion. Had this special knowledge informed the glance he gave her as he approached Minos with the recovered ring? Or was she imagining it all? Were they nothing to each other? A Cretan princess and an Athenian hostage—did nothing link them? *But he had looked at her with a kind of recognition.*

What could they tell her about Theseus, those slender, sad-eyed girls who gazed at him with so much awe, so much tremulous hope? What could those youths who so clearly patterned themselves after him tell her as they emulated (with varying degrees of success) his straight-

shouldered stance and his strutting, insolently confident walk?

From the moment she decided to help him, she became self-conscious about her role as obedient daughter. Sooner or later her own people would see through her. For instance, the jailor (who appeared to be asleep when she sneaked by him down the dank dungeon stairs) might reveal her duplicity at any time. She had hidden in the shadows and patiently watched him until his head finally nodded and his breathing became regular and unsuspecting. It was a small comfort to tell herself that he could not have seen her. Exposure could come from anywhere. She might even betray herself. When the Minotaur's wail reached her, she was stricken by doubt. Half of her sat in judgment on the other half, and each half found the other wanting. Part of her needed the Minotaur to exist; part of her needed to destroy him. As she stole to the Labyrinth late at night, the roar of her internal quarrel might have alerted the entire island.

The heavy Labyrinth door with its carved bull's head was never locked. It didn't have to be. No one cared to trespass on these dreadful grounds. When Ariadne first pushed against the door, it seemed immovable. I can't open it, she thought with agonized relief. But she had to open it. She had to test her plan. And with continued effort, she was able to get it open just wide enough to squeeze inside. Then it clanged ominously shut, and a sweetish stench enveloped her.

Daedalus, who built this bleak and haunting Labyrinth, must have patterned it after the road to Hades. Bitterness permeated the fetid air. She held her breath as long as she could. At last the need for even that air became overpowering and she breathed it in, grew accustomed to it, failed to notice how it poisoned the spirit, wondered if in time one's lungs grew more suited to it than to the pure air of a green countryside. Confined, for any length, to these narrow runs and dead ends, how could one not begin to mewl, to snarl, to move about on all fours?

She had tied one end of her yarn to the horn of the bull's head on the door. As she crept along, unraveling it, she began to pray. She prayed that it might be possible to explore the Labyrinth, its grime, its stench, its scuttling phantoms, its staggering suggestion of evil and, on returning to the palace, still be clean, still be beautiful, still be adored, still be able to find pleasure in a new gown, a new hairstyle, a new comedy by Aristophanes. All along she knew that her prayers were absurd—she whose safety had always lain in obedience.

The passages were so low in places, she had to crouch on her haunches and waddle along like a goose. Crawling would have been easier, but then her hands would have sunk wrist-deep in the filth. Fortunately these low sections soon gave way to places where she could walk upright. There she came upon a small pyramid of human bones, out of which two pale skulls leered. Fear cramped her heart.

If only she had never heard the Minotaur's lament. If only Theseus had not come. Then she might still pass as one whose thoughts did not offend and whose dreams caused no outrage. Now it was too late.

What if the remarkable lifeline of yarn snagged on a jutting rock? What if it tore, leaving her stranded? What if the Minotaur, ignorant of their kinship, devoured her in some crumbling nook? It might be for the best. Outside they would mourn her death and love her more than ever. They would grieve for years. But the yarn did not break. Nor did the monster seize her, though from time to time his dreadful breathing sounded so palpably close she had to stand very still and hold her own breath until he shuffled off.

A dungeon cell: ill lit, rancid, the rough walls filmed with moisture. The man locked inside was little more than a silhouette. She could barely make out his features as she pressed against the bars. *She* pressed against the bars—almost, one could say, as though she were trying to force her way in. They had not spoken before; but he had occupied her thoughts so constantly since that day at the sea's edge, she could fill in what she did not see from memory. He stood mistrustfully an arm's length away. She spoke rapidly, the words rushing from her. He *must* understand at once. *At once!* Every moment spent in explanation heightened the chance of discovery. He wanted some concrete proof, it seemed. She insisted he trust her, that he listen to her plan and take her yarn and dagger on faith. What reason did he have not to trust her? What chance did he have without her help? No chance. None.

How could he not see that? *She* was the enemy—that's
what he was thinking. At least that is how she interpreted his
guarded look, his questions.

Those in neighboring cells hunkered motionlessly in the
half-light. All that distinguished them from the shadows
were their eyes, which, like the sweat beads pimpling the
walls, reflected the playing light of her lamp. The effect
was of thousands of wary eyes watching.

With a skeptical air, he took the yarn and dagger from
her. "Will you take me with you when you sail from
Crete?" she asked, knowing that she could not remain here
if the Minotaur were killed. As Theseus was agreeing, the flame
of her lamp started to smoke. Beyond the smoke, he appeared
bluish and unreal. But—he was a real man. He held a real
dagger. It was a real dungeon in which they stood, real bars
through which they appraised each other.

There were so many preparations for the great day. There
were countless fittings for the silk gown she would wear,
the bodice of which could never be laced tightly enough. It
pushed her breasts seductively upward. The full-flounced,
lacily embroidered skirt emphasized the curve of her hips. It
might have been a bridal gown designed to whet the desire
of even the most reserved of grooms.

Minos sent her a tiny jeweled crown to wear on that day.
Perhaps he thought to make her his counterfeit queen. The
tyrant. She was honored and dishonored by his devotion:
pained that she was not what he wished and angered that
he wished it.

Minos, her father: the stiff-backed severity of his mien, the
weary circles gouged under his eyes, the sharp nose grown
(she saw with a pang) too large for the face, as if with the
lifelong objective of scenting out traitors. These were the
things, it seemed, that stirred both her love for him and her
anguish.

The dawn broke on a gloomy sky. If she could only stay
in bed longer, if she could only have her food brought to
her there, if she could only be dressed much later on by warm,
kind, unhurried hands—all might yet be fine. The secret
visits to the Labyrinth and the dungeon might yet be no more

than unsettling dreams. Everyone had such dreams at times. And at those times, dread always clung to the awakening dreamer.

She dreamed that the king was dead. His ghostlike form, with its closed eyes, its yellowed skin, its locked mouth, continued to hover in front of her when she awoke sobbing. Was his soul contained in that bolted-up form to which no one possessed the key? Was it alive behind that stony flesh? Was it beating inside that stilled heart? The implacable finality of its retreat seemed too terrible to bear.

Though the image of the dead king faded gradually as mist, the chariot of the sun remained hidden on that grim dawn—as if it were preordained that this would not be a day like all others . . .

Masses of people crowded the streets: noblemen and their ladies, bull-dancers, slaves, peasants, children. A scattering of dogs roaming through the mob caused small pockets of consternation: bursts of growling, of shouts, of cheers—all quickly subdued. Soldiers on horseback appeared. Their showy battle dress would have been dazzling on a sunny day, but under that brooding sky it looked dull and drab. The sight of these warriors would have been intimidating on a sunny day. Through their conquests, after all, they had made Minos master of the sea. But today, as they bullied their way forward, they looked like malicious children with their remorseless eyes, their witless belligerence, their eagerness for the death of the hapless Athenians. They acted like malicious children wielding wooden swords and make-believe shields.

Suddenly the confusion, the voices, the barking, the shuffling were stilled. The prisoners, flanked by guards, appeared in twos. With the exception of Theseus, they walked mechanically, without will or purpose. Fear gleamed on their faces. Were they truly doomed? Had her plan been discovered? Had the yarn, the dagger been seized? Their fear was infectious. It sped numbingly through her. Flashes of lightning whitened the sky. Hammer blows of thunder followed. Thunder mixed with the groan of the Labyrinth door being hauled open. Ariadne thought of the bones and the two sightless skulls that waited inside.

A blast of cheering shouts, screams, barks, the sound of horses' hooves. The Athenians were led to the wide-open mouth of the Labyrinth and it swallowed them up.

Ariadne followed them in her mind. Six youths and seven maidens came upon the heap of pale bones and stopped. They were trembling. Their eye sockets appeared as hollow as those of the skulls. Theseus inched his way all alone along a mold-crusted passage. Near him, but hidden behind a crumbling wall, a woman sat on the ground. Her legs stuck straight out in front of her. Her skin, darkened by grime, was withered to the texture of a dried plum. Her hair was a nest of Gordian knots that would never be untied. She had grown mad over the long sunless years and she laughed a jungle-bird laugh while at her breast a monster suckled.

It was as if Theseus had tied the end of the yarn she had given him not to some stone near the entrance but to her. As he neared the heart of the Minotaur's lair, she felt the tug and pull so strongly, there was no choice but to follow him there. She arose and stepped down from the dais. Were Minos to reach out and grasp her arm, were he to curse her, were he to call his guards with their fancy swords and feathered cloaks to bar her way, he could not stop her. That time was gone. Minos, her father . . .

He had always been there—like the palace itself, with its thick, strong walls that protected her every day and night of her life. Even when she did not see him, when she did not think of him, he had been as much a part of her as her own heart, which, unremarked sometimes for weeks, went on beating nonetheless.

He had been there—striding through the great halls, presiding on his throne, commanding his fleet, loving, grieving, eating, dreaming—before she even existed. He had known her when she was an infant. He had known her as she learned what warmth was, and cold, and also what hunger was, and satiety. He had known her when she was learning to take one tottery step after the other, learning to make words out of sounds.

That she had never known him except as king felt like loss. His love, like the jewels in his crown, gleamed real

but remote. A statue of him as a young warrior stood in the garden behind the palace. It may have been sculpted when he was the same age she was now. His face already wore a guarded expression, and one hand rested in readiness on the hilt of his sword. Yet the jawline, fuller than it was these days, lent him a kinder, less cynical look. What good, though, was the statue? What use? No sensate friend, no brother could be lured from its marble bosom.

Had he loved the young Pasiphaë when he wed her? Had he chosen her simply to produce an heir? What had gone through his heart when he discovered his choice to be the wrong one, when he decreed that his queen be locked out of sight with her monstrous son?

The years before she knew him sounded like they must have been the best in his life. The battles, the victories, the great banquets held on his return—they all took place before she was born. Those who had fought alongside him reminisced on occasion. They spoke of a man who was quite different from the somber and critical man she knew.

Lately rumors circulated (originating with mistresses? servants? no one seemed to know) of how he cried out in his sleep: frightened, wrenching cries; and how he slept with his sword at hand, and how he had once leaped from a sound sleep to draw his sword from its sheath although no enemy had entered the room and he was not in danger. Though such stories might have puzzled her once and she might once have disbelieved them, these days she understood how vivid, how murderous and profane the most incorporeal of specters could seem.

The drama inside the Laybrinth, the clash, the sounds, the fear, the delirium, the dying beast, the bloodied hero—so exactly as she had always imagined it—pained her in a way she had not expected. The monster she saw at last was far smaller than legend had painted him and was hardly repugnant. He had, she thought, a unique sort of beauty: lustrous blue-black fur, shapely muscles, a haggard, almost childlike face that imparted in death a weary innocence. Yet those long, curved horns (the tip of one quite bloody, the other one broken) had wreaked much anguish.

She asked Theseus about his wounds. They were scratches for the most, he told her. Only the one in his thigh gave him some trouble. The creature had gored him there just as he leaped onto its back. So she tore a strip of cloth from her skirt and fashioned a bandage for him. He put his arm around her shoulders for added support and they began to make their way back.

All the way out of the Labyrinth, she planned to ask for forgiveness. Once they emerged, she realized how senseless this was. Who would forgive her? Not the king, certainly. The Crete they returned to was not the Crete they had left. It was changed. Or perhaps it was they who were changed. The streets that had been so crowded earlier were deserted except for a beggar leaning against the city gate. As they neared him on their way to the harbor, this beggar turned out not to be a beggar at all but, rather, the king. How changed he was without his servants, his guards, his advisors, his host of followers around him! The gold threads in his cloak had tarnished, and the jewels in his crown were glass. What struck her in particular was how shrunken and pale he looked. She would have liked to say something kind to him. But she had broken his laws, and

so she passed him by with only a guarded glance and no farewell.

On the island of Dia, where they stopped to rest, the memory of how small and weak her father had looked touched her as the man had not. She sat with her back against a tree, some way from the others. They had built a fire on the beach. Someone killed a stag and they were roasting it. She catalogued the sounds: a man's voice, the crackle of fat, a woman's laughter, waves lapping the sand. They were happy to be returning home. It was a happiness from which she felt excluded, since it was from her home that she had fled. She thought of the old king, bent and thin, with a fake crown aslant on his head. The crown had slipped sideways and he seemed not to notice. Were she there, she might be tempted to set it aright. Her sadness over not being there was mixed with a strangely exhilarating joy.

What is she to make of the incriminating memories and the bewildering telltale memory gaps? Suppose that, taking her by the hand, I lead her through the labyrinth of shadow pictures? Can I present them to her in such clever sequence as to make their meanings sharp and clear? Will there still be time for her to say, "These were my secrets, these my sufferings, these my loves and losses"? Or does confusion reign indefinitely: the last bastion between dreams and realities?

CORONIS

THE FRAGRANCE OF THE MEADOW HAD BECOME UNFAMILIAR. IT was no longer that of clover and honeysuckle but, rather, of some more melancholy flora. Coronis followed the trail of broken grasses like Theseus the Minotaur's grim, baiting call. She had never seen the meadow looking like this: straw yellow against a mutinously dark sky. Like a child exploring a forbidden place, she was impelled onward by fear and an irresistible curiosity. How could a storm be brewing in this near-blinding daylight? She placed her feet carefully, one in front of the other. There was a sudden rustling near her, a rush of wings up past her ears, and the explosion of a bird's wild shrilling. It plucked a chill note in the whorls of memory. *Had this happened before?*

Something white lay just ahead. It was partly obscured by the waving grasses. Rags, she thought at once—as if she knew. Had she been here before? Had she examined these discarded rags, discovered their worthlessness? No, no; she could not have been here. The meadow stretched out beyond the rags (which were assuming a kind of shape—human? animal?) to meet a bulwark of purple hills to which the black sky was anchored.

A white bird, roused by her passing, flew high into the air. Before it glided back down again, the sky had stained it an inky black. It settled on the rags, which had in the meantime, become identifiable as a sleeping woman. It perched like a black curse on her pale breast and peered into her unguarded face. It's a crow, Coronis thought, and shuddered. She drew her thin cape around her shoulders more closely.

Something about the sleeper was disconcertingly familiar. Her eyes were closed. Even so, Coronis *knew* their color to be the wistful gray of winter clouds. She halted beside the sleeping figure. Better not bend down close. Better not waken her. With the crow's raw, ugly *caw-caw*, each faint line in the quiet, aristocratic face, each pore, each eyelash shifted into knife-sharp focus. *Better not gaze too searchingly . . .*

A ruby glistened on the woman's breast: *a glowing, darkening ruby affixed to her with a golden arrow.* Was that arrow really an arrow? It might have been no more than a shaft of sunlight. It might have been no more than a joke played by a laughing god. It might have vanished, like the sun, behind a cloud. It might have vanished with a teasing chuckle. Like Apollo, the sun god—always teasing . . .

Apollo, in his splendid chariot, whipping his white horses into a gallop across the sky . . .

Apollo, with his bow and his golden arrows that faithfully found even the most distant mark . . . *"But I can't," she had cried when he urged her to try her skill with them. "Can't?" he said. "Can't! There is no such word as 'can't.'"*

Apollo could pluck a dead flower from its dry root and make it bloom again.

Apollo.

Without him her life would have been a forest of shadows. Sometimes her love for him made her ache so intensely she could hardly bear it. And sometimes her love was as still and numb as if he were nothing to her; as if he were a stranger. He seemed to sense when the numbness happened—and was angry.

"The reasons for falling in love are infinite and mysterious," he said. "Love is like happiness that is simply there when we least expect it and has no connection with reason and need." She had just set a goblet of wine down in front of him and was pouring one for herself, mixing it with water. Whatever she answered, it would be construed as an affront.

"There is nothing mysterious about need," she said, watching his face flush and his eyes grow remote. "Need is what drives us to seek one another out. Need is one of the things that bind us."

"Do you actually mean to equate need, a symptom of base human weakness, with love, that most elevating, most god-like of passions?" he said angrily. "Do you actually mean to say you love me only because I can make your flowers bloom all year round?"

"Partly," she answered, with a suddenly racing heart.

In an even and coldly rational voice he explained that true love was not linked to such trivial conditions.

Knowing she had lost, knowing she had damned herself already, she steadfastly disagreed. She accused him of selfishness, of childishness, of willful ignorance. She clung stubbornly to the hope that she might quell his accusations with her own—only to discover yet again that she could not. Should she have led him outside to their garden, their rainbow-bright world, and showed him how his gift to her had been a gift to them both? Should she have persisted in the face of his denunciations? Should she have defended herself more vehemently? Should she have cried? Should she have beaten her breast? Should she have beaten his?

The young woman had been asleep in the meadow for as long as Coronis could remember. The problem was that her memory, which stretched back in sweeps and leaps some twenty years, had unpredictable gaps. How long had she been standing in the meadow looking at the woman, for instance? How had she come to be in that meadow? What had she been doing just before coming here? Had she been laughing? crying? gardening? napping? aimlessly humming a tune? Had she been sitting at her loom? Had she been taking a walk? Had she been gnawing at a ragged fingernail? Total and crushing was the darkness that severed minute from minute, memory from memory.

Waiting. That was it. She had been waiting. She had been sitting on the steps of their little house with its marvelous profusion of flowers in front and its weedy meadow stretching out behind.

A long time ago she had tried to pull up those weeds in the back in order to plant flowers there. She hoped to surprise Apollo by doing it without his help. But the weeds had terrifyingly strong roots. As she tore them from the loamy soil, blood dripped from the lacerated ends of those long, tangled ganglia. Of course, she reasoned, it must be the rich brown-red soil, still wet with a recent rain, that dripped from those ends. Yet alongside the best reasoning the sight was still violently repellent. Even if she had managed to conquer her revulsion and uproot all those weeds, she would have had so much bare ground to till, to fertilize, and to plant. Furthermore, would what she planted really grow? Her seedlings (those little threads of palest green, so lovely in their infant state of becoming) had too often sprouted only to dry and wither for no apparent reason. The weeds, if nothing else, flourished.

What she had been doing was awaiting Apollo's return from Mount Olympus. Waiting ... like a good and docile and obedient wife, although she had been outspokenly unhappy about his leaving.

"But you know they do expect me ... there are obligations... I must ..." he said by way of explanation.

He had not seemed at all reluctant to leave, which tainted her longing for him with anger. She was carrying *their* child in her body, but he had left carrying only what was his. I must stay here in limbo while he goes off to enjoy himself, she thought. He is selfish, ungiving, and uncaring, she thought. After obsessing in this way for a while and feeling no

better, she decided it was wrong to spoil her love with bitterness. However, despite her intention to forgive, this bitterness took shape inside her. It rooted and grew without cultivation. Unable to uproot that dark bloom, she blanketed it with forgetfulness.

Apollo was a god. When she was with him, she was almost a goddess. He said he loved her, and sometimes they were truly happy together. She thought of his flame-yellow hair. She thought of the tiny scar just above his left eye. She thought of how it pained her to imagine him being injured, though she knew nothing of how that injury had been incurred.

Before he left he said, "The crow will bring me news of you. It's not much of a flight for him from here to Olympus. He can bring me word of you every day."

That was all quite true. What good was it, though, if the news only traveled one way and the crow brought her no word of him?

Be that as it may, it was wrong of her to be angry at him. Wasn't it?

Hadn't it always been wrong as long as she could remember?

The sight of the young woman asleep in the meadow stirred an elusive pain. Something was wrong. Was it the position she was lying in—one arm twisted back under her, as if someone, taking hold of it as she lay down, had tried to keep her upright? It could not be comfortable to sleep this way. Coronis resisted the impulse to touch her, to straighten her arm, to brush the creases from her gown, to arrange its folds over her white legs, which were, she noticed, startlingly exposed. Perhaps it was this nakedness—the vulnerability it implied—that pained her. Asleep, one was so defenseless.

Since Apollo left, she had been unable to sleep through a single whole night. The child turning in her womb would waken her. Or the shadows creeping heavily about in the dark. Or nothing.

The sounds of the night could be so frightening . . .

She would lie very still so they could not hear her: those crickets with their love calls and answers; those phantoms beating the air with hollow-boned wings; those wolves whose howls echoed from mountain to mountain for an unnaturally long time. It seemed to her that, for all her twenty-odd years, she was still like a child, overwhelmed by a child's sense of loss on perceiving how many of its wishes would never come true—and how love, precious though it was, was imperfect.

Years before she met Apollo, she had fallen in love with a man named Ischys. He had ridden into the courtyard of her father's castle on a gray horse. She saw him from her window and was impressed by his powerful physique. He looked big enough to wield the heavy thunderbolts of Zeus. The sight of his strong face and Herculean body thrilled her. Surely there was nothing in the world he feared. It seemed to her that if he took her in his arms, she would be transfused with his strength. If he looks up, she thought, if he sees me and smiles, that will mean he is mine. He did look up. And he did smile. But he never lifted her up beside him on that prancing horse. They never rode out of the courtyard together. They never lay in each other's arms on a night when the moon, a luminous guardian, might have touched them with magical light. Yet, somehow, all these things did happen in the instant he smiled.

That same day he disappeared from her life. What remained was the memory of his smile, beguiling and intimate as a secret between them. She willed him back to her. She willed him to be her lover. She clasped her own shoulders, her own arms, to reclaim the feeling of his imagined embrace. Years passed and he did not return. Occasionally she heard his name spoken. In time it took on the aspect of a stranger's name and ceased to produce that tug at the heart, that quickening of the pulse.

She grew to believe that memory had enhanced him. There was no man like that. Had he returned to her, she would have inevitably discovered an assortment of cruelties, coarsenesses, and uglinesses in his nature. Thus his absence spared her the death of her love. By degrees, she became grateful for this harsher of mercies. It is quite

possible, she thought, that he snores resoundingly at night. Or that he passes wind in his sleep. By now, too, he has probably grown grizzled and worn out. His beauty has been eroded by so many days spent in battle, so many nights spent in trenches, so many years never really sleeping because a soldier, always wary, cannot afford the luxury of dreams.

What dreams might the lady in the meadow be dreaming? What raptures might she embrace? What handsome warrior? Can she keep him handsome forever in the magic circle of her arms? Can her dream kisses keep him from fading?

Coronis did not think much of her own dreams. They were puffs of air. Their mosaic of perfumes, music, glorious castles, flights through the clouds—all receded at dawn. Why measure such transience against the enduring realities of the world? One might as well measure shadows (which grew or shrank with the hour) against the bodies that cast them.

She loved Apollo as completely as her human soul would allow. She loved him despite the small deceptions that this love accrued: the misunderstandings, the sacrifices, the little deaths, the little sorrows, the petty disillusions. She loved him as naturally as life itself. Why, then, must anger sour her heart? He loved her too.

Only . . .

He demanded she desire what *he* wished her to desire, imbued her with moods and disguises he fancied, with secrets that had nothing to do with her own.

"Women don't love me," he told her. "Women have never loved me. And so it's hard for me to believe that you . . ."

"You are my life," she always answered, and he always misunderstood. He insisted that she conform to his vision of her, that she fill in his uncanny gaps. One night she had a dream in which he addressed her with a strange foreign name. He had mistaken her for someone else, but she could not convince him of it. He accused her of misdeeds, although he was not specific. He behaved with a subtle cruelty that became quietly alarming.

Apollo never tired of recounting the many tales of his still-born loves: those stories which, because they were so well known, were more real than all her tendernesses. There was

the story of Daphne, who, fleeing from him to the river
bank, chose to be turned into a laurel tree rather than become
his bride. There was the story of Cassandra, who refused
him despite his golden hair, his fiercely blue eyes, and the
gift of prophecy he promised her. There was the story of
Marpessa, who preferred to age and die alongside her mortal
lover rather than enjoy immortality as his mate.

"So you see . . ." he would say wearily. It meant nothing
to him that Clytie, with her slim waist, her long, shapely
legs, her firm little bosom, gazed after him so longingly with
dark, sorrowing eyes. She was a silly, vapid girl, he said,
whose fawning adoration simply annoyed him. He callously
changed her into a sunflower so that her round, yellow
face, with its halo of yellow petals (forever turned toward him
in any case), might worship him less obtrusively.

"Sometimes I wonder what you would do to me if you
considered me obtrusive," Coronis said.

"Why should I consider you obtrusive?" he asked.

Coronis knelt beside the sleeper. Who was she? The answer danced at the periphery of her mind. She touched the
clear, warm brow with her cool fingers and again was struck
by how much a shaft of sunlight could resemble a quivering arrow. But—surely it was only sunlight.

What cruelties her beloved Apollo inflicted, she mused, in
his quest for love. She had, for as long as she could remember,
trusted the gods to be fair. How long could she remember? It
was hard to say at which point memory became a source
of confusion rather than clarity.

Sometimes she did not love him at all. My husband, my
love, my whole life, she would think, and feel bitterness,
feel emptiness, feel distance, feel nothing. They could make
love pretending this brought them close when in fact it
underscored the trouble. They had been separated by the
whole long day, from which he returned oddly changed.
They remained separated by a curiously insatiable need.

"How do we look to you down here when you're up in the
sky driving your sun chariot?" she asked. "Like toys? Like
ants? Like specks of dust? Like anything at all?"

"When I'm driving, I look at the horses," he said.

"What do you think about when you're driving?"

"I think about the horses. They would know at once if my mind wandered and would instantly take advantage to charge off the path." It was an answer that told her he resented her question. He protected his thoughts from her. He defended his distance.

A scene flashed through her mind: a man stepping down from a shining chariot to which fiery horses are harnessed. He wears a gold panther skin that leaves his burnished chest bare. Chariot and horses radiate the reds and lavenders of a sunset. These smoldering hues reflect off the man's skin as off metal. A quiver of arrows is strapped to his back, and he holds a bow in his left hand. A woman, very small and white against the darkening landscape, appears to glide toward him from a great distance. She is almost transparent, almost a ghost. As she throws her arms wide to welcome him, he fits an arrow into his bow, whence it disappears as if by magic. The bow string shivers with a melancholy twang.

The ruby, affixed to the sleeper by a shaft of sunlight, grew larger. Painfully red, it touched a distant, answering pain that had no discernible source. The pain might therefore belong to Coronis or to someone else. Somewhere a crow cawed, "Ischys! . . . Ischys! . . . Ischys! . . ." Could that be?

Apollo had wounded her in some obscure fashion.

Oh? And how had he done that? Accusation per se hardly proved a case.

Apropos of nothing, she remembered a yellow lightning flash, sharp as an inhalation of flame. But she also remembered his joy in being with her, his pride in her beauty, his son growing daily more real in her womb. Still the wound—distinctly, there was a wound—was so raw, so hurtful, so rank with distrust, a kind of madness bloomed from it. Madness might explain the rifts in her memory.

What had she so *madly* wanted of him?

That he deny he could ever leave her.

What had he wanted of her?

He was often nostalgic about the moment they met, when, emerging from a shadowy room, she'd been so dazzled, so

nearly blinded by the glowing sight of him. Without exactly saying so, he took umbrage at her refusal to remain dazzled. He did not consider that her eyes had adjusted to the radiance in the meantime. How could she, even to please him, live every hour of her life with dilated pupils?

Their little refusals to please each other went nearly unnoticed. Each seemed to ask only that which was reasonable. Each seemed to deny the other only that which made a kind of sense to deny. Each spoke of love believing to have said all there was to say while neither of them were truly reassured. How much does he really love me, she would wonder. And he would think: she is no longer dazzled by me. Therefore, there must be someone else.

Coronis disliked the crow she'd seen feeding on the maggoty intestines of a rabbit. She complained to Apollo of its disgusting habits and he told her how loyal it was to him. It perched on his shoulder. It fetched the twigs back to him that he threw. It brought him news from around the world. It loved him unreservedly. It was his friend.

"Crows are scavengers," she said. "They feed on filth."

He laughed at her indignation. Why shouldn't the friendly white scavenger perform his little tricks to amuse them?

Not *them*, she pointed out. It amused only *him*. He disagreed. The crow was fond of them both. She accused him of preferring it to her. He laughed again.

When the crow sang prettily, she threw it crumbs. When it produced its grating *caw-caw*, she strove to ignore it. He seemed unable to distinguish between its songs and its clamoring. Once it soared into their valley cackling wildly about a fire. "Flee! Flee!" it shrieked, as if the entire valley were about to be engulfed by an inferno. This hysteria turned out to have been over no more than a small campfire built by an old shepherd to keep himself warm.

"I wish that crow had been roasted over the fire," she said.

"You give this nonsense too much importance," he answered. "Crows are naturally flighty."

Was it actually possible to burn the miserable bird to death? she wondered. Or would it doggedly rise, an odious phoenix, from its own ashes? To avoid quarrels, she forced

herself to call the crow's spying "interest," its galling chatter "the overtures of friendship," its insolent presence "companionship." It made itself at home in their garden and ate the seeds she planted. She wondered what the normal life span of a crow might be.

Apollo left for Olympus and appointed the bird their personal messenger. "It will bring me news of you," he said, thus chaining her to a fidelity she had no wish to shed.

He left without saying how long he'd be gone.

Wasn't it so, Coronis remembered arguing, that Daphne had been struck by Eros's lead-tipped arrow just before she spurned Apollo? Hadn't that very arrow ensured her indifference to him? Hadn't her rebuff therefore been predictable? Apollo shrugged. That had happened long ago and was of no present interest to him. Coronis persisted. What of the fact that Cassandra had taken a vow of celibacy? Shouldn't that have forewarned him? Shouldn't he have known in advance that she would not welcome any man's approach?

Coronis threw scraps of food to the crow daily which it wolfed down straightaway. It apparently did not fear being poisoned by her, although she regularly fantasized little scenarios of murder. Ah, the pleasure of consigning this pest's corpse to the earth where it might, at least in decomposing, do her garden some good!

Coronis puzzled over the resemblance (more obvious from some angles than others) between herself and the sleeper. What *was* the connection between them? If she could only ask her . . . if she could only waken her . . . She was quite tempted to but did not dare. Was this because the domed sky had become so unnaturally black that the meadow, in contrast, appeared bone white?

She used to wonder why her love for Apollo left her heart hungering. Wasn't love food? Couldn't food fill the belly completely? How, then, could love fail to fill up the heart? True, a sumptuous meal could be enhanced by a sip of nectar beforehand or a sweet at its conclusion. Why might human hearts not be as adaptable as human bellies? And why was it that when he put an arm around her as they were falling asleep, she felt as though he cut off her breath? Why was it that she was often so dejected in his company— as if his very presence somehow poisoned the air? Because I am ungrateful, she thought. Because I am foolish.

She became self-consciously loving: ran to greet him whenever he returned, saw to it that he always had his favorite foods to eat, let her eyes linger on him with seeming longing. But thoughts of Ischys slipped between them with increasing frequency. It plagued her that this alien love could thrust its way unbidden into her life. Was all the apparent affection she showed Apollo in some way fraudulent? Would he see into her wretched heart and know its burden? He was withdrawn and humorless in the days just before he left for Olympus. She asked what was troubling him, and he denied being troubled.

Am I a traitor? she asked herself. Am I faithless? It was a bleak consolation to know her behavior was virtuous while she lusted after a man she dared not even look at without a veil modestly covering her face.

She might never have seen Ischys again. Fate placed her at the same window from which she'd first seen him when the clatter of horse's hoofs sounded in the courtyard below. She might not have looked down. But she did.

. . . and caught her breath sharply. He looked exactly as she remembered him all these years: his full, black, curly hair, his lustrous beard, his strong, confident warrior's body. He had been older than she then. Now he seemed just about her age. Had he moved through an enchanted stream of years that exacted no dues? She wanted him as intensely as she had long ago, and the discovery of this old need—so fiercely alive—was wrenching. Will he look up and see me? she wondered. All that they might have been to each other, all the intimacies, triumphs, and sorrows of the life they might have shared, sped through her mind at once. But he did not look up.

She did not see him again. Yet his image was a guilty secret she carried back home. When Apollo embraced her, it slipped between them like darkness.

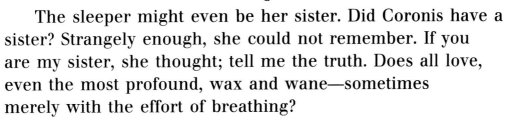

The sleeper might even be her sister. Did Coronis have a sister? Strangely enough, she could not remember. If you are my sister, she thought; tell me the truth. Does all love, even the most profound, wax and wane—sometimes merely with the effort of breathing?

There! Over there—something there at the crest of that hill! What is it? A flash in the distance distracted her and she forgot what she was thinking.

Time would reduce her treacherous secret to nothing. She had only to wait. But while she waited, Apollo (of whom statues were sculpted to celebrate his beauty, to whom sacrifices were made, for whom odes were written) grumbled that his body had grown soft as a boy's or a woman's. He challenged her to deny this. He called her denials obvious lies designed to placate him. It was clear, he said, that there were others she preferred to him.

What she should have done was cry, shriek, tear her hair, scratch her face and body bloody to prove that she did not lie.

"Everyone lies at one time or another," he said, and recalled a particular instance when to avoid an argument she had pretended . . .

Yes, *pretended*—which was hardly the same thing as lying. Nevertheless, he stood firm. Clearly he was right. She grew silent, hoping that in silence at least she would have a defense. To insist too much on her innocence was itself suspicious. Silence would vindicate her, she hoped.

Instead it led him to say, "There, you turn away so quickly. You are suddenly so pale and quiet. That proves I'm right."

A memory, stark and alarming, leaped from ambush to catch her by shocked surprise: Apollo, slipping the quiver of arrows from his shoulder and flinging it across the room with a crash of anger. Golden arrows scattered on the ground, torch light balefully flickering on their shafts.

She had started sleeping badly. Long periods of wakefulness stretched between short, exhausting bouts of sleep.

"Why can't you sleep, though?" he asked. "There has to be a reason. There's always a reason."

So she invented reasons to satisfy him, knowing they weren't wholly true. Many things happened for no special reason. There was no reason for the dark circles under her eyes, no reason for the troubled glances she threw at him, no reason for the sudden sick pain that would strike at the center of her being.

Now, in the meadow, she looks up and does see him in the distance—although she can't be absolutely sure. It is only a movement she sees, only a sparkle that might be light glancing off his chariot, or the ruffling of golden manes and tails in the wind, or the flash of hooves. But it *must* be Apollo returning from Olympus at last. She has scanned the heavens for him so often, so long. She has wished so dearly . . .

At night she would awake in tears because she was only a woman and not a goddess. She'd awake in anger because she would age and he would not. Angrily she said, "Yes, there are others more handsome than you. Adonis, for instance. Everyone knows he is the handsomest of men. And Hercules is stronger than you, even though he's only a mortal." Then, wanting him to stay (he had already turned from her), she added, "What difference does any of it make? You have surely seen plenty of women more beautiful than I." No, he hadn't, he told her. No woman was ever more beautiful to him than she.

With that reassurance, her anger turned to sadness. His accusations bore the painful note of truth. She *had* failed him. She *had* wanted another. There was no pardon for that, and the only atonement lay in self-condemning silence.

Had that been a shooting star? In broad daylight? A shooting star to herald his return? A shooting star to shoot down lovers? A golden star to shoot down dreams? Coronis seems to remember a woman in white running toward the flash, the dazzle, her arms thrown wide in greeting. She seems to remember how the star shot through the hot summer air and struck the woman's heart which started to bleed.

It is impossible to stanch the blood drawn by a star and the woman, faltering in her headlong rush, dropped first

to her knees and then fell asleep. The *caw-caw*s of a crow rose like uneasy laughter.

How Coronis suffered over her make-believe lover! How she cursed herself for surrendering to the embraces of a phantom, cursed herself for seeking a hold on nothingness, cursed herself for never having told Apollo how insubstantial phantom loves were, how much less they were than the lightest summer breeze! What she had told him on one of his returns (having prided herself on not thinking of him at all for an entire afternoon) was, "I never realized how possible it was to be happy without you."

There he is! He is only a speck in the distance, but there is no mistaking the sunset glow of the sky as his chariot comes down. At last, she thinks. She will hold him hard and real in her arms. Tears spring to her eyes. Her cheeks burn. She will no longer betray him with phantoms, no longer be sad. Once they are together again, she will be safe. She will learn how real he is under her touch, how loving he is under her kisses, how beautiful he is under her hands.

Her whole body watches his approach. Her feet grow ready to run toward him when she begins to remember that she had already run toward him. With her arms thrown wide to embrace him, she had already been crying out his name when his arrow—flashing, bewildering, white hot—struck her. She begins to remember how the dark, comforting sleep slowly filled her and pushed out the pain.

After so many days and weeks, he is coming back to her at last, is tearing down the sloping meadow as if to outrun his fateful arrow. Echoes fly, sting, wail, bound back and forth between this scene and her disjointed memory of it. He curses the white, tale-telling crow, turning it dead black for its treacherous assurances that Ischys and Coronis were lovers, its guarantees that Ischys was there with her, that it was Ischys running toward him across the meadow.

Apollo sinks down beside her, his eyes wide with grief. He clutches her to him. He covers her still face with kisses.

From moment to moment her body grows cooler in his fevered embrace.

What if love is less than enduring? What if it is like some exquisite jewel that once possessed must be quickly hidden lest it provoke the enmity of a jealous god? What if it is no more than a prettily plumed bird, marvelous in flight—and in flight, only too vulnerable to the hunter's arrow? What if, once struck down and left to rot on the dirt-brown earth, scavengers come to peck at its eyes and tug at its pale green entrails?

What wisdom can be drawn from the dire fate of Deianira and Hercules? They fell in love with each other's beauty. They swore oaths to each other that they could not keep. They lay in each other's arms whole nights long but were not—with all their love—immune to the deadliness of fleeting time.

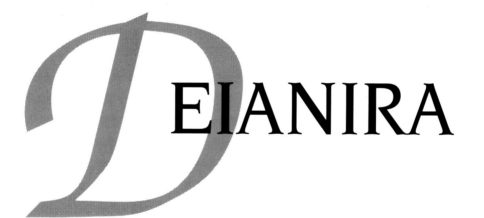DEIANIRA

ONCE EVERYONE KNEW HOW WILDLY HE LOVED HER. IT WAS IN the way he looked at her, spoke to her, spoke about her. It was in his constant desire to be with her. It was in his challenging Achelous for her hand—Achelous, who was a god after all, while he, Hercules, despite his astonishing strength, was only a mortal.

They had stopped touching a long time ago. All that was left to caress now, it seemed, was the past. The present included the long dining table *without* him at its head, the

hum of chatter transformed into silence by her entrance
into a room, the inert horizon to which she looked for a sign
of his return, and their unshared marriage bed, from
which she wearily arose ever later with the passing days. As
for the future looming ahead, this is what she saw: a
woman growing ever more transparent until, at last, people
could look through her as easily as if she were not there.

They had stopped touching . . . that sort of thing happened,
she told herself. Life was not meant to be a constant
fulfillment.

But he had been splendid in that clash with Achelous
when the river god, changing into a serpent, had wreathed
him in great crushing coils. Yet serpents, even a gleaming
god-serpent like Achelous, were nothing to Hercules, who
had already strangled serpents when he was a tiny infant.

He grasped the writhing Achelous just behind his fanged
head and would have strangled him soon enough if the
river god had not changed shape again. In an explosion of
sparks and smoke, the serpent became a bull. Hercules,
ever undaunted, broke an ivory horn from his head.

He had risked his life for her! for love of her! she told and
retold herself in vain. No single memory worked the magic
of soothing her desolate heart. Could she trick it into silence?
Could she distract it, as one could a restless horse by
throwing it some hay? Why not just conclusively tell it: "HE
LOVES ME!"? Why not just dam up the angry tears that
altered nothing?

She could only imagine that this oppressive and enduring
despair came from something very simple, very ordinary,
very much in keeping with the process of nature itself. Despair began as a tiny, innocuous seed that, once tucked
away under the brown earth, put forth a knife-thin stalk one
day.

Hercules had conquered the lands of King Eurytus. Iole
was Eurytus's daughter. Princess Iole. Deianira could
imagine her with ease: the smooth forehead, the delicate eyebrows, the alert, deceptively innocent gaze, the softly
molded cheekbones and chin, the crafty mouth so beguilingly
poised on the beginning of a smile. Who was to say that

she was not, at this very moment, awaiting Hercules in her tent? Who was to say that she was not propped against silk pillows, her skirts pulled coyly up to reveal parted thighs?

Iole was nothing. She was one of the many spoils of war. Not more, not less.

And what was Deianira?

Was she an oracle that she saw events taking place far away, in another land, in a time of siege? Was she a ghost that she could prowl about in the minds of others, hearing their thoughts? Was she a madwoman? Was it only in her distraught head that she was wearing out, growing insipid and unlovely to him? Was it not the act of a madwoman to blame her husband for being a man? What should he be if not that?

She would not blame him. She would not torment herself by believing she could read his mind. Misinterpretation was all too possible. His long absences need not betoken a waning love for her. Hercules was a warrior. Therefore he warred. Therefore he marched against Eurytus, king of Œchalia. In war one killed. And one took captives. Acts spoke plainly enough. It was a great misfortune that they could not be plainly understood.

"We have been married for years," she said to herself. "He has gone many times, but he has always returned. I have borne his sons. We have shared much of the best and the worst. Should I begrudge him the trivial comfort of a concubine? Should I seek to dictate his passions any sooner than I should seek to harness him, like a horse, to my carriage?

"So, this concubine is a princess? It means nothing. I too have royal blood in this aging body. I too have been called beautiful, and many men have courted me. These days it so happens that a relentless sadness—like illness, like night—depletes me. It is hardly surprising that I want him here now. I want to draw strength from him. And comfort. And that measure of joy—however mixed with grief—that the gods, in their capricious apportionings, have allotted me."

Who was Deianira?

She encountered herself (quite by accident) while wandering from one day to another. "No!" she cried at once.

"That can't be me! There's more gray in that woman's hair than in mine! That furrow between the brows is too deep! Those lips are too starved and bitter to be mine! Only the long neck, the slender waist, the graceful hips might be mine. Only the white, inviting arms . . ."

He made no secret of the other women. There was no need to. They meant nothing to him. Or—they meant no more than a shiny goblet raised to his lips, drunk from, and flung down. So he claimed.

So life taught her—along with its other hard lessons: that the victorious took the spoils, that desire was fickle, that love aged badly.

She was a resistant student. Once she wrested his heavy sword from its sheath and, staggering (she needed both hands to hold it), dared him to take it from her, to thrust it into her heart, to finish her quickly, mercifully, rather than in that cruel, excruciatingly slow way with his distances, his absences, his indifferences.

"To endure pain is to grow strong," he had answered, wrenching the sword from her and thrusting it back into its sheath. Then he turned abruptly and strode from the room. His receding footsteps echoed for a long time afterward. Later (she was lying on her back, diagonally across the wide bed, her eyes dry) she heard laughter outside. He might be laughing at her. He might be laughing because he'd already forgotten her. It might not be he who was laughing. It might not be laughter but the chirring of insects. It might be warm summer rain pattering against the courtyard stones. She could not tell.

Pain could very well make you grow stronger, she thought. But pain could also ravage you. Pain could destroy you.

There had to be some way of bringing him back by the very intensity of her need for him. Would totally abandoning herself to despair do it? Would drinking herself insensible accomplish it? Would taking every passing man as a lover win him back? What of refusing all sustenance and becoming daily less and less of herself until she was indistinguishable from the shadows?

She wandered from window to window, stopping at each to gaze out for a time, as if each slightly altered view of the world outside might present a suggestion not previously

thought of. But she was too wretched to see anything new.
It was as if the gods had erased all suggestions beforehand.
At last she sat down in front of her mirror, picked up her
brushes, and began to curl and arrange her hair. She tied and
retied ribbons in it until each last ringlet was acceptably
in place. Then she changed her gown to one that was tightly
laced at the waist and fell to her feet in many fine folds.
It complimented her shape and the sway of her walk.

Love.

As a child she thought of it as a treat that would one day
be hers. As a young woman she thought of it as the answer
to all her questions. These days she thought of it, rather, as a
terminal disease inflicted on hapless sensate creatures by
the tainted arrows of a ruthless Eros. It sapped one's strength.
It perverted one's reason. It subjected one to the most re-
fined agonies.

Love: it poisoned the whole human organism. And what
better antidote for a poison could there be than an alter-
nate poison?

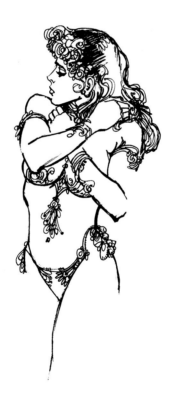

Though he accused her of being jealous, of being petty
and spiteful and even vicious, she disagreed. A more accu-
rate appraisal of her flaws (if such they were) might be that

if stabbed, she bled, and that, moreover, she was not a readily forgiving woman. She distrusted those seemingly selfless types who absorbed insults and injuries without a whimper. She thought them bloodless and false. What he mistook for jealousy and the rest was, rather, an agonized sense of having been violated.

Only half-alive in his absence, she took comfort in remembering certain details of their times together: Hercules, silhouetted against the firelight, removing his armor almost leisurely—as if they had so much time yet, an infinity of time together. And she undoing the fastenings of her own gown, her half-bare body accented by shadows ...

He still drew the accolades he always had: *Ah, Hercules, the strongest, the bravest of men!* Praise warmed him like light from the sun. Even she could sometimes be warmed by it when he was near. But his absences had become periods of night throughout which a terrible loneliness held sway.

Because he was a man, her woman's fears and dreams were uninterpretable to him. He could not understand how he had become special to her because she had given herself to him, entrusted herself to him, accepted him, not only into her being, but as part of her being. Even she was staggered to see how that innocent acceptance bound her to him with a force beyond oath and duty.

And now he loved Iole.

He had slain Iole's father and brothers in order to have her—hardly a gentle courtship. Clearly the blame fell on Eros and his treacherous arrows. What good, though, was knowing where the blame fell? The sickness ran its twisted course until it vanished or veered off into madness.

Was he mad?

All these years she had chosen not to think about how he had slain his first wife, Megara, and their children as well. Although he loved them. Although he grieved. Although he did not eat or sleep for days. Although, in an orgy of atonement, he pleaded with death to exact its dark and final justice. Ironical that his penitence (the twelve years of servitude to King Eurystheus, for whom he performed the twelve brutal labors) brought him fame and adulation.

What if he had slain her that day when, grasping his

sword, she'd goaded him on? Would that have increased his glory as well: *Hercules, the conqueror of kingdoms, of terror, of guilt, and of women's whims?* That instant he'd swept the sword from her hands, there had been murder in his eyes. If he had killed her, he would no doubt have cried, "The gods must know I'd never intended this!" And no doubt he would have thought: I'm rid of her now. Heroes were apt to be honored for the very acts other men were condemned for.

He had once again pillaged a kingdom and reduced its populace to empty-eyed corpses. No doubt at this moment they were being dismembered by hungry dogs. He planned a sacrifice to Zeus in celebration. He sent Lichas to her that he might fetch a ceremonial robe to wear on this occasion. As she looked into the guileless face of the young messenger and heard his request, an idea came to her . . .

She dug the small flask of blood from its hiding place under the crushed linens, the old sandals, the bits of ribbon where she'd buried it a lifetime ago. It had aged in its secret hiding place. The surface of the flask was worn, and it had somehow suffered a deep scratch near the top. Once it had been filled with water and strapped to the girdle around her waist. That was when, as a new bride, she'd set out with Hercules on their journey to this place. Nothing untoward would ever happen to her, he'd promised, as long as she was at his side.

The flask was filled with blood now—that dark, poisoned blood of the Centaur Nessus. It seemed to grow hot as she held it, and she laid it on the floor at her knees lest it burn her hand. Then she sat staring at it as the afternoon blended into evening.

Some sins were considered almost virtues. They were naturally approved of and easily forgiven. Some sins, on the other hand, were unforgivable. These must be atoned for, without recompense, a lifetime long. Yet one could not always distinguish beforehand between the forgivable and the unforgivable sins. There was the blood of the dead Centaur, hidden away for so many years, and now . . .

So long ago that there was almost no connection between then and now, she believed she needed only to be beautiful in order to be desired. She needed only to smile in order to be happy. She needed only to acquiesce in order to be loved. If she did not cry, she would not be sad. If she did not rage, she would not be angry. "Deianira is a true princess," all said of her.

Princes came from everywhere to win her. None, however, were princely enough to suit her father, King Œneus. I am lucky, she thought, that my father is a good judge of men, because I would be incapable of making the right choice. But who, after all, should see into the souls of men better than a king? A princess is too readily taken by a gallant gesture, a flattering phrase, an attractive face.

Achelous came to woo her. He came in the shape of a bull, with his animal stench, his quivering muzzle, his frightening horns. He came in the shape of a serpent with alien yellow eyes that had slitted pupils. He came to her also as a Minotaur, half man, half bull, with a thick, wet, lolling tongue and blue smoke pluming from his nostrils. If he sought to charm her with these loathsome shapes, what could they hope to share that might pass as joy? she wondered.

"Achelous is a god," Œneus said, pleased at the prospect of a deity as a son-in-law. She smiled to quench her disgust and never tried to learn what else a smile might quench. She'd discovered only lately how alone and how desperate she could be behind a smile. She envied those who simply demanded what they wanted: her father, her husband, even the strange and revolting Achelous. She supposed their wants to be more valid than hers.

Perhaps she should never have started smiling. Or never have stopped. But she had stopped, and, look, she was close to madness. She was thinking mad thoughts, murderous thoughts. She was thinking of how the beautiful sorceress Medea had slaughtered her own children out of just such madness, just such rage. She tried to tell herself that this was a temporary aberration, that it would pass. But before, the rumors had only been of women without names or faces, women who could not really be felt to exist.

Husband and wife.

What did that mean? The words might refer to two stones that had come to lie side by side on the ground. They might further imply that these stones had lain there for ages and seemed matched well enough, although a careful look would disclose that they had failed to make any impression upon one another, not the slightest molding, smoothing, or fitting-together of the touching sides.

There is the rising temptation to do something violent: to kick them out of their slumber, to force them into life, or else to bring a hammer down on them and smash them to bits. Violence, though, because it is easily misunderstood, is best discharged in secret.

She remembered the long-ago battle Hercules fought with Achelous: her champion's energy, his blazing eyes, the murderous blows he dealt the god . . .

She sat with the flask of blood before her and remembered the crossing at the river Evenus after their marriage. She and Hercules had been traveling across the rough country toward the place that would be their home. Now and again he had carried her across smaller streams, holding her in his arms so effortlessly that she shivered with the realization of his strength, his warmth, his concern. When they came to the Evenus, they found it foamy and swollen with the rain of recent storms. It rushed by, carrying tree branches, broken bits of wood, and the occasional floating corpse of some small drowned beast. How could he keep her safe in that turbulent crossing? How could he prevent a broken spar or a swollen corpse from crashing into her? He was ready to face any danger for her, fight any evil. At that time, he was ready to die for her. But the river was too deep, too perilous for him to risk her.

She remembered Nessus, the Centaur, and how his black hooves struck the ground, making it tremble, beating out a rhythm against it like the thunder beats of a raging heart. She could still see his brown, burnished coat and the thick black mane of his hair rising in the wind as he galloped toward them.

Everyone had heard about Centaurs: about their savageries, their drunken stampedes through farmlands and

towns. They were known to slice a man's throat as casually as one might pluck a ripe fruit from its stem. . . .

Nessus offered to take her across, offered his broad back for her to ride on. Could they trust him? Of course he had been taking travelers across the Evenus on his back for hundreds of years. Then too, what choice was there? She thrust away the visions of anonymous bodies grown slick with gore under his sharp hooves. She refused to think of the stolen children, their high, thin, terrified sobs fading in the dusk. She pushed off the thought of the cold, braying laughter that was said to sometimes echo down from the hills.

Nessus appeared to be so helpful. Surely he was not like those other Centaurs. Thus Hercules lifted her onto the creature's back. She still remembered with chagrin how the mud from her sandals had spattered his tunic as he swung her up.

He loved her. Yet he never—even at the beginning—told her so. It would have betrayed a weakness, a femaleness in his nature. What he did to show his love was to slay her suitors.

She sat on the floor in front of the chest from which she'd taken the flask, and wondered if it was even possible for events to have taken any other turn than they did.

Long ago, Hercules plunged into the Evenus and swam toward the far bank. Long ago, Nessus stepped into the river, proceeding stride by careful stride until the foamy current reached his belly. Long ago he reared and spun about on his hind legs to gallop back up onto the bank. She felt the enormous power in his legs, felt them churning vigorously under her as he galloped out of the water. She cried for him to stop, to let her go. They tore across the stony land toward the tree-grown hillocks among which they would soon vanish.

Hercules, who was already on the far bank, did not dive into the river to swim back. He did not send curses and threats in pursuit. If his feet lacked the swiftness of the Centaur's hooves, his arrows did not. He fitted an arrow into his bow and let it fly with a hum of vengeance. It missed her head by a hair's breath and sank deep into her captor's back. As he collapsed, she scrambled off him. He struggled to get on his feet again, but it was clearly useless.

"When Hercules no longer loves you ..." the stricken Centaur had gurgled as blood flowed from his mouth. "Save my blood in your flask—keep it from the sun, keep it in a dark place, keep it hidden. A few drops of it rubbed on a garment he wears will restore his love," he murmured. *When Hercules no longer loves you* ... Had his vision become so acute that he could see her future? *When Hercules no longer loves you* ... Once the bitter suggestion had been planted in her mind, what choice did she have but to greet each day with the onerous question: How many more days? How much time do I have left before it happens? Would she be so despairing now if despair had not been suggested then?

What should the Centaur have seen as his life bled from him? What more fitting words should he have gasped with his failing breath? Should he have, rather, confessed his sins to her? For what purpose? She could not have absolved him. Should he have spoken of the tragedies of life? Of its inequities? its beauties? its simplicities? its pitilessness? All this would have required time. He had to be brief. And so he spoke of the future ...

It had been naive to hope the dreaded day would never come, that she could stave it off with puerile smiles; that she could prevent the inevitable by not asking questions, by not listening to rumors.

What of his first wife, Megara? The story went that he had never meant to harm her. He had been blinded by madness when he murdered her. He had not seen a woman but a demon when he struck her down. He had truly loved her. But— wasn't hatred the dark side of loving?

If he was so wholly innocent, why did he do penance? Why did he indenture himself to the cowardly King Eurystheus for twelve hard years? Why atone for an affliction (and its concomitant crime) that was willed on him by the gods? Because Megara had not always compliantly smiled? Because she had enraged him with her wants and wishes? Because his wishes had always been sane, so it followed that hers, when they opposed his, had to be insane? Because, if she promulgated injustices and insanities, murdering her had been an act of self-defense? When he thrust his sword

through her throat (so the story went), he'd seen her as a vile, snarling creature with venomous red eyes and serpents for hair.

Deianira wept. She feared using the Centaur's blood to recapture her husband's love. Was she wrong to plot so desperately? To want him though he no longer wanted her? All her life she had listened, obedient as a child, to the dictates of men.

Tears blurred her vision and fell on her hands. I must stop this, she thought, or my swollen, reddened eyes will announce my misery to the world.

As a child she had heard many stories of gods and goddesses, heroes and ladies. She no longer remembered the details of these stories, only their endings. They all had the same ending. The heroes and their ladies were always torn from each other's arms by dreadful circumstances. Sometimes a lady was kidnapped or given as a slave to a cruel master. Sometimes she was imprisoned or slated for sacrifice to a flame-breathing dragon. Whatever happened, the lady always bore her pain, her fear, and her loneliness with uncomplaining courage. And the hero always rescued her at the last possible moment, after which they would live together happily forever and ever.

It must be nice to live happily, she would think sadly—as if she had some presentiment that this happiness that should be her due would inevitably elude her. The soft covers that blanketed her at night, the warm broths she was given to drink on chilly days, the sunlit rooms, the breezes redolent of spring, the comforting presence of her nurse—all that should have left no room for apprehensions. But it was as if something evil lay in wait at the edges of her vision, at the far ends of hallways, between the cracks in the walls or the floors. Flitting shadows seemed to watch, to listen. Loneliness often closed frighteningly on her even when she was cared for and protected. She wondered if loneliness was synonymous with illness? One had to be so cautious. One could never be cautious enough. And if one dared to break any of the rules . . .

She seemed to tremble when she opened the chest to re-

trieve the flask. She held her hands out in front of her and was amazed to see how steady they looked. The trembling was invisible.

She thought of the dead Centaur. The river that he had crossed and recrossed so often had swallowed him, lost him, lost the taste and the smell of him, although his bones, picked clean by now, must still lie somewhere on its stony bed. She thought of how brightly the sun had shone on that arid landscape. It had made every rock, every bare tree, every distant hill stand out with painful clarity. She thought of the Centaur's beastly roar as he whirled and splashed toward the near bank. She'd clung to him as tightly as to a lover, but only because she'd been so afraid of falling into the roiling, racing water. And she screamed for him to let her go.

"What are you screaming for?" he laughed. "What are you afraid of?"

His rancid breath in her face, and his thick arms imprisoning her, meant he would destroy her. There was no escape. Then, miraculously, Hercules' arrow thudded solidly into his back, and its poisoned tip emerged redly from his chest. The arrow had just missed her head.

She was strangely moved by the thought that love, even at its height, could harbor a seed of death. One was curiously locked to one's fate by such laws.

The flask had been meant for water or wine. An ordinary flask. Its scratched surface yielded no hint of the magic it held. Nor did any telling odor arise when she opened it and held it to her nose.

The Centaur had said, "When he no longer loves you, pour my blood on one of his garments. As soon as he dons it, his love will be rekindled, its flames more impassioned even than now." Those words were so faint, she would have missed them had her face not been so close to his, her ear so close to his gray lips it might have been a poor, wretched kiss he imparted at the last.

Could she trust him? Why should he have wished to help her? Why should he have wished her anything save tragedy, save awful retribution? Had there been a touch of kindness in his villainous nature? Did the sweetest dreams pave the way to disaster? Did sinister truths hunker behind her desperate hopes? Did the discovery of one's blindnesses always come too late? Should she tip the flask to her lips, drink the unholy blood, and so have the answer once and forever? It would be simple enough to do. The smallest movement of hand and arm would raise the flask, tilt it, let the dark ooze flow down her throat.

She had wrenched herself free of the dead Centaur but not of his prophecy, and not of the hope he gave her: that terrible, seductive hope . . .

Hercules had conquered the kingdom of Œchalia, where he was now preparing to make a sacrifice to Zeus. He had sent his servant Lichas to her with the order to fetch a garment for the occasion: something splendid, something ornamented with jewels. When she needed him so terribly, when she needed him just to be there, he sent Lichas in his stead. Was it truly the sacrifice for which he wished a new garment? Or did he think, rather, to appear more handsome in Iole's eyes?

To be the wife of Hercules seemed glorious to every woman save the wife of Hercules. Possessing wealth, she had no need of wealth, save that which his love gave her. Thus she gradually grew poor with the passing time. How had that happened?

There were expedient explanations: men's need for variety, their joy in conquest, and so on. These explanations explained nothing. Real faithlessness, after all, could not be that readily perceived. It was an act that took place secretly, in the heart. For only the heart was susceptive to real transgression.

She never loved him more than in the hour of her rage. She never loved him more than when she spread his jeweled tunic out on a table and smoothed its folds. Deep scarlet in color, it would never show the blood she rubbed carefully along the hem and into the seams. Yes, he would come back to her. Yes, he would want her again. Yes, she would drive all her rivals from his mind. He would get down on his knees to her. He would swear his love to her and she would coldly say, "What do you know of love? What do you

know of giving? of trust? of waiting? of the anguish of always waiting?"

Loathing her anger, her misery, and her awful need of him, she gave Lichas the bloodied tunic. Her clear gaze and her smile were lies, as were her kind words for Iole. How cleverly the mind and the tongue converted dread feelings to more palpable fare. She could hardly wait to hold him close again—real and alive and hungry for her.

But Lichas had been gone only a few hours when the pleasant murmuring of her hopes turned to a gasp of pure horror. The cloth she had used to smear blood on his tunic had turned to ashes. The odor of burned flesh rose from it in awful prophecy. She had doomed Hercules and doomed herself. The room shuddered. The walls grew indistinct. She backed away from the dreadful evidence and staggered through the tilting, shifting hallways. She had to flee . . . to flee . . .

Halfway to the palace gate she discovered that she was moaning—a dry, toneless bleat like that of a dying sheep. She loved him despite all their failures. She loved him despite their unshared bed. She loved him without hope and without reason. She loved him with an avalanche of tears. She loved him because of all the years that linked them. As she ran toward the gates, the horizon appeared to darken with burgundy blood.

Once, it seemed, they had invented love. He had sworn (with such an easy laugh) to love her always. What had it cost him, that oath, that innocent's promise? He had passions and fears and dreams and regrets she knew nothing of. They existed in spite of her, and perhaps to spite her; and perhaps, too, they had nothing to do with her.

He planned a sacrifice to Zeus.

Should she, too, appeal to Zeus? Throw herself on his mercy? Or was it too late?

And when had it become *too late*?

The boat that was bearing him home was still far from shore when she smelled the fiery stench of him rising toward the red sky.

They rushed to tell her, to spare her no color, no sound,

no grim detail of how, after Hercules donned the tunic, he
began to behave most strangely. They told her how he stepped
up to the altar to make the sacrifice and grew suddenly
pale. They told her how he tore at his clothes in a frenzy, how
he howled like a beast when the cloth came away from
his chest with scorched pieces of flesh. They told her how his
skin blackened and split and his veins burst with sizzling
blood. They told her how, with flames leaping down his arms,
flames snapping from his fingertips, flames crackling in
his eyes, he called the quavering Lichas to him, seized him
by the legs, spun him round and round, and hurled him
into the Euboean Sea with such force that he was turned to
stone. They told her that he still lived, despite his torment,
and that he was, at this moment, returning to her along with
his curses, his loathing, his agony, his terrible pleas for
death. And, finally, they told her how she, frail and a woman,
had broken him, unmanned him—Hercules, the mightiest
of men.

Her love for him was no shield against such accusations.
Her love, born in the dark marrow of her bones and suffus-
ing her body as surely as the poison invaded his—that love
sustained her no longer. Despair, ravenous and mad, devoured her. Despair devoured all hope, all future. Despair became her god. There was no place to lay her head save on
despair's bosom. There was no place to lay her heart save on
despair's altar.

What remained to be done was clear.
The past in which she had lived for him and through
him—that past in which she had laughed and wept because of him—was severed forever from any future. Despair
had weaned her of tears and of laughter, and what was a
future bereft of these? Warmth had vanished from the world.
Love was fraudulent.

If she could only retreat in time to the moment before
she'd spread the monster's blood on the tunic. What miracles she had wished from that blood, what preposterous joys!
If Despair would but hide her, forgive her, pity her. But
Despair, that exacting god, bestowed absolution only through
death.

She fled past the columns, the statues, the friezes with
their cold sculpted scenes of rendezvous and farewells.
When she reached the sanctuary of her room at last, she
barred the heavy wooden door. Then she lifted his sword
from its rack on the wall and dragged it to their marriage bed.
True, cuckoldry was a bitter solace when virtue was all
that tied one to life. With that fierce steel lover invading her
flesh, she would cut the thread.

. . . *Wild and pitiless Medea! She refused to grieve over the faithlessness of her Jason. She murdered the woman he would have left her for instead. And she murdered their two sons to rob him of heirs.*

After their flight from Iolcos, after so many days and nights together, after more than ten years of a genuine partnership during which he had come to know her so well: to know her foibles, her powers, the barbarousness of her justice, and above all, to know the intensity of her devotion to him—he forgot all the promises he made to her at the start. How callous, how imprudent of him to have gone to Creon, the king of Corinth, and ask for his daughter's hand in marriage. He might have known how Medea would repay such deceit. He might have been chastened by the foreknowledge, but . . .

MEDEA

EVERYTHING IS PREORDAINED: HEIGHT, WEIGHT, STRENGTHS, flaws, loyalties, defections. All allusion to "free" choice is misleading.

From childhood on, Medea could raise her little arms toward a dark sky and make the stars burn with a heightened brilliance. She had the power to warm frozen rivers and liberate the myriad little lives caught there by winter.

When she got older, she could summon the most hideous of scaly beasts simply by imagining its presence. She could sprinkle it with powdered herbs and turn it improbably beautiful. It was not through any special virtue that she earned such gifts. She was born with them. Medea, passionate and savage from birth, might as readily sacrifice all that was dear to her in the name of love as turn on that love in vengeance.

Jason and his companions just appeared in her father's court one day. They had rowed up the muddy Phasis River, disembarked, requested an audience with King Æetes and announced that they had come for the Golden Fleece. Medea had been touched by the blatant innocence of that request. Heat reddened her cheeks as Jason—splendid with determination, sunlight flashing golden from his armor—told how he must bring the fleece of his uncle Pelias or the latter would deny him the crown.

Am I in love? Medea wondered with a suddenly pounding heart. She heard her father agree to give over the fleece if Jason could yoke his fire-breathing oxen to a plough and sow his huge field with dragon teeth. The king sounded deceptively courteous. He had a curious repertoire of voices: the caustic, fastidious voice he used with condemned men; the gritty voice, roughened by shouting, that he used with his men-at-arms; the light, playful voice with which he spoke to his young son, Absyrtus—a voice that constricted her heart each time she heard it.

She listened quietly to the king's conditions, her hands folded in her lap, a look of polite interest concealing her thoughts. The rapacious oxen with their brass horns and hooves would trample Jason. The dragon teeth would sprout from the earth's womb not as fragile green plants but as warriors. Furthermore, that mad army of mindless men would slay her Jason. They would leave his body unburied. In time death would swell his battered corpse and make a monster of him who in life was so beautiful. She raised her hands to her eyes to block out the visions. The only thing she feared in the world was losing him.

Medea walked along the path through the woods. She

passed in and out of the moonlight, vanishing and reappearing. The mating cry of tree frogs, silenced by her approach, resurged as she moved on. It trilled and reverberated like love itself: capricious and elusive, an echo, a mirage. She paid no attention to the tree frogs.

She had always been fearless—unlike the meek and tedious Absyrtus. Even so, she was merely a daughter to Æetes, her future circumscribed: a brood mare, wingless. At the age of this adored and quaking Absyrtus, she had already made pets of dragons. Small and delicate as a child, she spun enchantments to make herself grow tall and strong. She kept a list of injuries she had suffered, determined that no threat go unchallenged, no insult unpunished. This much she understood: a curse, once uttered, could destroy.

Medea met Jason at the edge of the woods on the ribbon of beach that separated the trees from the murmuring sea. Because she stepped from the blackest shadows onto the moonlit sand, she seemed to him to have appeared by magic.

"Will you help me?" he asked. "I need you."

Jasonnn . . . His name was a melody sung by the shore-lapping waves. It was a pulse beat of yearning deep in her bones. It was a dancing, a dreaming . . . Jason. He knew of her. He had heard . . . What had he heard, though? And from whom? Her whole life up to that point had been spent on the island. Not once had she left it—which she would have to do if she helped him. She would have to flee. She would be banished, exiled, damned . . .

But the strong survive damnation.

And those in love at times tramp indifferently over others.

He took her hands in both of his. His smile denied his misgivings. "I have heard you are a witch," he said pleasantly.

He was a perfectly ordinary man except for the nerve-lengths of excitement his touch launched under her skin.

"Witch . . . ?" she repeated. "I would rather you called me 'enchantress.' Witches are too often hated—as though all their spells were evil. As though they could not perform real miracles, bring real happiness."

He was not listening to her. He was looking at her, holding her hands, but he was thinking of the oxen. He was thinking of their size, their enormous strength, the orange flames pluming from their dark muzzles, their long, pointed horns. He was thinking of the warriors that would spring from the dragon teeth: how they would outnumber him, how they would turn on him, how they would slay him—not swiftly, but cruelly, methodically. He was thinking of the serpent guarding the Golden Fleece: of its long forked tongue, its curved and deadly teeth.

"What chance does a man have in the struggle against monsters?" he asked, as if it had just occurred to him that Pelias had sent him on this quest to be rid of him for good and all.

"Men are misled by the obvious," Medea said. "They place too much faith in the superiority of size and numbers. It is mainly by little secrets, by inventive strategies, that the balance can be shifted. What you must do tomorrow is this . . ."

The next day the oxen stood frozen, intent, appalling, in the vast meadow. Only the puffs of flame and the smoke curling from their nostrils distinguished them from inanimate stone. The dreadful heat of their breath blackened the grass all around and blistered the hide of a nearby dog. It galloped off with a shrill yowl. But Jason had oiled his skin with the lotion Medea had given him, and the terrible heat felt no worse to him than a warm breeze. He approached the oxen, stroked their necks, slipped the heavy wooden yoke over their heads, and harnessed them to the plough. Then he drove them back and forth across the field and sowed the yellowing dragon teeth.

Did Æetes suspect Medea's duplicity already then? Hard to say. His narrowed eyes registered what might have been wry amusement. On the other hand, a phantom suspicion may have tugged at him. He did covertly glance at Medea as if to assess her reaction to Jason's initial success.

She was hardly eager to face his rage without the insulating distance of time. To hear him curse her would be unbearable, she thought. Yet it was not his anger she feared, but his grief.

Across the flat expanse of the plowed field, the earth humped into little hills—a graveyard of hills. Each one rose exactly above the place where a tooth lay buried. As the hills

swelled, the ground rumbled and cracked. From each hill an armored warrior pulled himself forth. They might have stepped from a damned man's dream with their clenched fists and soulless faces. At the sight of them Jason's danger-chasing companions turned sickly white.

Stillness gripped the onlookers like doom, like heat. Jason knelt and picked up a stone. As if on impulse, to see if the creature would feel it, he threw it at the closest one.

And if the creature does feel itself struck? If blood does trickle down its cheek? Jason had always thought of death as something he might choose or reject as one chose to advance or retreat in a skirmish. How naive that was. Terror made itself at home in the bravest heart. The silence of his audience throbbed in his ears. If he could only choke off that silence, he could gain control of the quaking in his knees. He remembered the ambiguity in Medea's eyes when she instructed him about what to do today . . .

The stone struck a warrior square on the cheek. Blood appeared. The man looked about, perplexed. Then he swung his sword and struck his neighbor on the shoulder. This one, misinterpreting the source of the blow, struck the man behind him and sliced off an arm. The one-armed man in turn split open a head. Before long, the fearsome army sprung from the dragon teeth had decimated itself.

"So you see," Medea said to Jason later, "fate and magic are interrelated, as are truth and lies, or reason and madness."

A superficial gash above the left elbow was all Jason had sustained. In the excitement of victory and congratulations, he had hardly felt it. One day he would finger the old scar, remember the shock-wave of pain when the spear tore his flesh and remember his flash of surprise because the oil that inured him to the oxen's flaming breath had not protected him from spears too. Or . . . ? One day he would wonder if this unexpected wound had been a kind of warning. He would remember how quickly it had healed once she ministered to it. And how he had promised to marry her knowing it was impossible once they returned to Thessaly. She was a foreigner there, and the law forbade marriage with foreigners.

The Golden Fleece was guarded by a dragon that never slept. All day sunlight smoldered in its reddened eyes, and at night a menacing starlight glimmered there. It spat and reared as Jason approached. Medea had given him a sleeping draught to use on the dragon. When he was as close as he dared go, he flung the vial and watched it smash against the thick scales. At once the hissing beast collapsed. Its breath slowed and its terrible eyes closed. If Jason hadn't known it would awaken shortly, he would have sworn it was dead.

This was the moment to seize the fleece and escape. Yet he stood, the color slowly draining from his face, as though mesmerized by the sleeping dragon. In some sense, he too seemed to be asleep, held by the ghastliness of the dream. Then he felt Medea's hand on his shoulder and heard her telling him to flee. The urgency in her voice pierced his trance. He turned to her. There she stood holding little Absyrtus by the arm, a curious smile on her face. She must have had a frightening grip on the child, for tears welled up in his eyes.

Medea would always remember the first time he kissed her. His men had been rowing furiously for some minutes. Colchis lay far behind them on the mute horizon. It appeared to be no more than a rutted strip. The constant wind had chilled her, and his lips were warmer than she'd expected them to be. She wanted to lose herself in their warmth, their texture. But Æetes had already set out in pursuit. His boats, so much lighter than the *Argo*, glided toward them as swiftly as poisoned arrows. If we are caught? trapped? brought back down the Phasis to Colchis . . . ? She refused to follow that thought through to the end. It must not happen. Their love for each other gave them too much reason to stay alive. If only Æetes might some day forgive her . . .

To live always at Jason's side, to see him crowned king, to make him great—that vision was too golden for any sin to tarnish, any crime to destroy. It was as he kissed her the first time that her plan to save them from her father's vengeance took dark and terrible shape in her mind. If Æetes could only see beyond the traitor in her . . . if she could only see beyond the enemy in him . . . But death *was* commonplace, and murder often the only means to an end.

Absyrtus, heir to the throne of Colchis, sat limply propped against the *Argo*'s hull. A whimper of fear slipped from his lips. Once she had envied him their father's love. Once she had despised him as a weakling. How strangely that antipathy now resembled the pangs of love. She took him below the deck, away from the others. He became giddy with fright. The motion of the ship together with her purred reassurances seemed to relax him. He listened so attentively to her, it struck her as novel that a brain might be formulating thoughts of its own in his little head. And that his puny body might actually be composed of flesh, of warm blood, of articulate bones not all too different from her own.

She reached for the dagger she had under her robe.

Did anyone see them? Was anyone near? She looked quickly about—as if it mattered. As if it would not all be discovered soon enough. Discovered—and eventually condemned. But she had no choice. The river moaned against the *Argo*'s oars.

At the last moment Absyrtus started to scream: raw, staccato explosions of fright, which her dagger cut off and sliced into chunks of silence. Her hands were stained red. A fluttering inside her turned to ice.

She flung the gory chunks into the *Argo*'s wake along with the memory of how her little brother had trembled against the blade, trembled violently, like an earthquake at first, and then less and less until he was perfectly still. Now the king had to abandon the chase and gather those chunks. Let him collect them and count them and recount them until they added up to his son.

Homecoming. The quest for the Golden Fleece ended. Jason was back, victorious. Crowds. Celebrations. Feasts. Sacrifices made to the gods. Incense burned on the altars.

They had been there less than a week. Jason should have been happy and content. Yet he went about with a drawn face, a burdened mien. What was the matter with him? What could he be lacking? Wasn't all Iolcos singing his praises? Of course there was the vexing business with Pelias. That graying schemer had gotten the Golden Fleece and still refused to crown Jason king. However, that seemingly was

not what troubled Jason. He claimed to have hardly given it a thought.

"What is it, then?" she asked him.

He looked angrily at her, as if the answer should be obvious, and said, "The fabled fleece that I risked so much to win is nothing more than the yellowed hide of a long-dead ram." Did she think he had gone in search of it only to win a crown? he went on. No, he had done it for his father, to please his father, to make him proud. Did that sound so unusual?

His father had not joined the festivities. His father had heard nothing of the cheers, the adulation. He barely seemed to recognize his son. Such was the dreadful alchemy time worked on the living. This man who had once been big-boned and powerful, who could devour the entire flank of a deer at a single sitting, could barely eat these days. This shrunken man could not move from bed to chair unaided. This decrepit relic, once he was seated in a chair, did little more than gaze benignly into space.

When Jason brought the fleece to show him (how glorious, how luminous it looked in the sunlight, though it was not real gold and had even begun quite noticeably to shed), the old man's only response had been a vague smile, hardly suggestive of pleasure. Jason had spent half the morning with him, telling him of his adventures, telling him of the dangers he'd survived, of the men he'd lost, and, of course, of Medea, of her beauty, her talents; of their love. "It seemed to me," he said to Medea, "that if I talked long enough, he'd have to hear me, he'd have to understand."

The frail, ruined figure of his father bound Jason to such improbable sadness. "All we lose in the process of living teaches us nothing about loss," he said. "I am as unreconciled to death and dying as if I had never witnessed it."

"He is not dead," Medea said.

"No, that's true. He can still breathe. He can still swallow some bits of food if they are placed in his mouth. No doubt he can still feel pain if he is struck."

She studied him tenderly; the slope of his shoulders, the tilt of his head, his eyes invaded by grief. She reached out and brushed the hair from his brow. "Tell me what you want me to do," she said.

"What I want . . ." He hesitated. "If only you could . . . If only it were possible . . . If you would restore even as few as ten years of his life to him—even if it means taking ten years off my own life in exchange. That's a sacrifice I would be more than willing—indeed, I'd be joyous—to make."

"My poor Jason," Medea murmured after a moment's silence, and then embraced him. "I could not bear to reduce, even by a few minutes, the precious time we still have together." Jason's distress pained her even as it endeared him to her. Men were distinguished from one another by the things they grieved for, the things they cherished. His love for old Æson was her love as well. She too, she suddenly found, would despair greatly to lose him.

The full moon was a round yellow eye, a Cyclops eye, planted in the center of a black heaven. It lent a pale phosphorescence to the trees, the houses, the hills, the fields. Medea stood barefooted beneath its scrutiny, her arms raised, her thick hair loose and flowing about her shoulders. She had forsaken her own father, but Hecate would help her. She was not afraid. Though she was not of Æson's flesh and blood, he would be her father reborn, the father Æetes had never been. Her heart warmed when she thought of him listening to her; when she thought of him talking to her about his innermost feelings; when she thought of him asking her about her dreams; when she thought of him showing her the pink, lucent scars of his old wounds.

She knelt on the ground. After a moment, she threw her head back and uttered a cry that seemed to be torn from her bowels. Leaves stopped rustling on their branches. The night hum of insects faded. Life inside the neighboring houses grew still. The stars began to burn with an audible crackle in eerie harmony with her cries: *Is man the natural issue of babes? Is age the handiwork of youth? Is death the last invention of life? How can I reverse the order? What must I do? Where must I go? What do I need? Am I bold enough? Am I cunning enough? Am I wise enough? Nothing in this world is impossible once its mysteries are fathomed . . .*

The stars flashed and sang to her. The stars were worlds of silver fire. The stars rained magic down on her. She caught it in the cupped palms of her hands. She closed her hands into fists and held it tightly—silver fire.

She pressed her clenched fists against her eyes and imagined her chariot. It was small, ornamented with precious stones, and was drawn by an ancient two-headed dragon. This dragon flew higher and faster than any bird. It perceived the invisible. Its long talons were sharper than any sword. When she opened her eyes, her dragon and chariot stood near a cluster of trees. She went to it, petted both of the dragon's heads, climbed into the chariot, and picked up the reins. Then they rose up over the trees and flew off to the land where the special herbs grew that the stars had told her about.

For nine days and nights she wandered through forests and along river banks that no human being had ever seen. She was lonely for him. His absence was a tangible void that she filled with thoughts of their future happiness. Once her magic had restored Æson to them, their happiness would last forever . . .

Hecate spoke to her from the water, and from the moonbeams, and from the waving reeds along the shore. "Take care to keep him always hungering," Hecate whispered. "Men do not lust for that on which they've glutted themselves."

"You have always guided me well," Medea said. "And I have faith in your wisdom. But you speak of Jason as if he were like other ordinary men."

An owl hooted and a tiny creature, invisible but for the thin path of trembling reeds it made, scampered through the marsh. A moment later the owl, no more than a phantom, cruised by, dipping low to the ground. A cry, like a brief spasm of fear, sounded and was silenced.

Hecate continued. "Is this man part of you? Part of Medea's body—part of her spirit? Live with your love awhile. You will come to see how unlike you he is. How ordinary he is. Alas, you may even come to see him as your enemy."

"I cannot question what you say," Medea answered, knowing Hecate's power of prophecy. "But you have not gazed into his deep-brown eyes, not studied the grace of even his smallest gesture: the turn of his head, the raising of an arm—whether he is advancing, sword in hand, on an armored foe or approaching, unclad, the bed of a waiting lady. You

don't consider the splendid breadth of his shoulders, the fine texture of his skin, the provocative hardness of his body.

"I have but to look at him with desire for desire to flush his cheeks also. Oh, at times he might pretend not to understand what I want. But all the same he'll permit himself to be wooed, captured, held, and lovingly coerced into the compromising embrace. He will roll onto his back as naturally as a cat and expose his belly, all tanned and rippling with muscles. He'll surrender to my mouth, my hands, my body, as casually as any feline offering itself up for its mistress to stroke.

"It does occur to me that by loving him, I have made myself his servant, and that I may tire of this role someday. Still—*enemy*? And even if that should happen, I would regret neither the sacrifices I made for his sake nor my bloodiest deeds. True, man does imbibe, with his mother's milk, the predilection to smite his enemy. But you, my mother, suckled me on the ambrosia of enchantment. Thus I am not bound by the common rules.

"And if, after all, I am misguided? If my love does turn ugly one day? I can no more choose not to serve him now than the blind can choose to distinguish one color from another. What I must do does not frighten me. It only reveals the motifs of my life with increasing clarity."

When Medea had gathered all she needed for her youth-giving elixir, she summoned her dragon and chariot once more and returned to Iolcos. No one was allowed to greet her on her return lest the spell she was weaving be mitigated by their mundane concerns. Neither did she enter the palace. Though she herself had insisted on this reception, it felt like ostracism to her. She stood on the hilltop overlooking her new homeland and wondered to what extent the present foreshadowed the future.

Her new home . . . It was as foreign to her as she was to it. The memories of Colchis, of her childhood, all belonged to a past she had renounced. And because of all the years they'd spent speaking the same language, living within the same walls, celebrating the same holidays, mourning the same deaths, she suffered with the thought of her father's anger. Æetes reviled her with good cause. Yet for Jason she would commit all her sins again. She willingly suffered for Jason. Jason, whose image ever and again floated unbidden behind her eyes. Jason, who owed his life to her. Jason, who needed her.

She built an altar to Hecate on the hilltop. She hauled the stones and mixed the mortar herself. When it was finished, she selected a black sheep from the herd that was grazing on the hill and tied its legs together. Then she laid it on the altar and slit its throat. The blood was drained into a bronze cauldron and mixed with wine and milk and the special herbs she'd collected. She lit a flame under the cauldron. When the brew began to bubble, she added dew collected at sunrise, the heart of a wolf that had lived for thirteen generations, the skeleton of an eagle to whose ossified wings the feathers still clung, and many more things that would forever remain secret. Then she stirred the mixture with a dead olive branch.

All night long she stirred, she chanted, she wept, she shouted. She grew feverish. She grew insensible to weariness and the passing hours. She was transported by the very spell she wove as by one long ecstasy. The dead olive branch turned green, and just as the sky blossomed with dawn, it sprouted a single perfect leaf. Then two. Then three.

Medea sent word for Æson to be brought. He was carried up the hill to her and placed, like the sacrificial sheep before him, on the stone altar. Then the servants withdrew, descended the hill, and disappeared behind the castle walls. Medea stood motionless until they were gone. She gazed at the moribund man as if to memorize the withered contours of his face. At last she drew the dagger from her girdle, bent to place a kiss on the dry lips, lay the blade across Æson's throat, and pressed it into the flesh with sudden force.

The old blood drained slowly and thickly from the former king. When Æson's veins collapsed upon emptiness, she filled them again, pouring her magic brew into the wound she had made and into the mouth she had kissed. Soon the gray body, already chilled and stiff with death, began to warm. It began to show a touch of color in the cheeks. Just as the leaves had appeared on the olive branch, so Æson's thin

white hair turned full and dark. His parched flesh grew supple. His fragile, emaciated limbs filled out. All signs of morbidity dissolved. Transformed into a man of thirty, and vigorous with health, he opened his eyes.

Æson sat up. He looked about. He looked at himself, at the length of himself. He clenched and unclenched his big hands with wonder and no little perplexity. Medea stepped back so as not to distract him from this discovery of himself. As she watched him—her creation, her triumph, the manifestation of her skill, her power—a wistful sadness caught at her. She wondered if this gift of sorcery, so potent when matched against the laws of nature, was any match for the vagaries of a man's love.

"Have patience," Pelias had said to Jason about the matter of crowning him king. "I am old. I don't have much longer to live. When I'm gone, this will all be yours."

Medea, however, had no patience. "That kind of reasoning is closer to insult than to logic," she cried when Jason told her. Though there once was a time when she might have been content to wait, content to live simply with Jason, content to endure the commonplace travails of that shared life in exchange for the pleasures and comforts it could bring—that time was a murder ago. And it was before she had tasted the rapture of power, before she'd observed the awe in which others held her, the trembling that seized them in her presence.

The theme of murder intrigued her; the uncanny ease with which it could be committed. Thus she shaped a plan whereby Pelias' own daughters would be eager enough to cut his throat. Such morbid irony held considerable appeal for her.

Did crimes fade with the memory of them? Did they become less real, less terrible in time? Or were all crimes, even forgotten ones, noted, counted, remembered somewhere? Was killing Pelias the best means to an end? Perhaps. And perhaps not. But every moment given over to doubt might cost dearly. And it could not hurt for Jason to witness how she dealt with Pelias. Let him understand the vengeance she could exact. So Hecate predicted he would deceive her? With her own dark skills, with her knowledge of human greed, with the strength of her will, Medea would forestall that prophecy. Oh, Jason might, on occasion, want to make love to another; he might dare to imagine how another woman might feel under his body, and what little cries she might utter. But to actually pursue such a conquest ... No!

Pelias's daughters were pretty enough in an ordinary way. They vied constantly for their father's attention, which— occupied with pomp as he was, and with the companionship of his generals, and the flattery of his advisors—he had little time to give. His callousness, far from discouraging them, seemed to excite their shows of affection to ever- heightened degrees. His moods, his pains, his forgetfulness, his increasingly frequent spells of insomnia worried them greatly.

"I am getting old," he would remind them when they broached these concerns. "Each passing day, each passing minute, brings me closer to death. There is no altering the matter, my children, by turning your heads from it."

Now it was whispered in the hallways and behind doors and on the stairs and, finally, it was spoken about openly how the dying Æson had so incredibly recovered—not simply his health but also his youth. How could this have happened? How was it possible? "Medea" was the name repeat-

edly heard. "Medea" was the explanation. Medea, after all, was a sorceress. And still, the whole idea was preposterous, said the more pragmatic. Let ignorant folk believe what they liked. A more probable explanation was that this young man passing himself off an Æson (and bearing a remarkable likeness to the real one) was in fact a bastard son, disclaimed and unheard from all these years. Likely enough he had murdered the old man, and now he maintained . . .

With all the gossip, the speculations, the adamant beliefs and disbeliefs on the subject, it was natural that the girls became curious about Medea. They found her most intriguing—not in the conventional sense, as the elegant, soft-skinned ladies at court were intriguing, but in the arresting manner of a cobra: sleek, dangerous, amoral, her gaze curiously hypnotic. Added to this was the hope that she could— no, rather that she *would*—cure their father's old age and his pains.

How had Pelias wronged Medea? He didn't know her. He was a stranger to her. Yet the fate she planned for him was as harsh as if he had been an errant lover. She knew well enough that the people of Iolcos would condemn her for what she plotted. She did not care. How curious are the ways in which we call down judgments on ourselves, she thought.

Was it actually love that beat in her breast as fiercely as her own heart? That night when Jason embraced her, she had been almost tempted to laugh, almost tempted to push him away and cry, "What kind of farce are we playing that we try to fool each other with kisses? That we embrace and pretend thereby to have bridged the distance between us? We are too separate, you and I, our purposes too separate, our sensibilities too separate."

At the height of her love, she knew the propensity of love to wax and wane. One day it was there, full and real; one day it was gone, replaced by a baffling nothingness—and then, ingenuously, it was there again. What, on knowing this, was the thing to do? Ignore its inconstancy? Ignore the foreknowledge of loss and pain? Hold to appearances? Trust appearances to convince? Trust appearances to inform realities? Trust appearances?

Did Jason have any idea of her gruesome plan? He must have had some inkling when he saw her in the company of Pelias's daughters so frequently. When he saw them whispering and laughing together; saw them wandering off together in the fields; saw the strange little bouquets of weeds and grasses they brought back from their wanderings; saw the sickly black ewe, clearly the oldest in the flock (it was amazing how the poor creature could still get around, wobbly and arthritic as it had become) transformed, after a brief disappearance, into a young lamb again. There was no mistaking the lively little lamb's identity. It had the same patch of white above the right eye that the old ewe had.

If he suspected something then, and surely he must have, that would have been the time for him to voice his displeasure—his acute displeasure, as it turned out. After the thing was done and could not be undone, it was a bit late for recriminations.

She could have dispatched Pelias with poisons or with spells that would have snuffed out his life so naturally, not even he would have sensed anything amiss. But she had a taste for grim drama. She did not want to miss the fear quickening in her enemy's eyes. And he did die with his face frozen into livid despair, his eyes bulging, the corners of his mouth drooling blood-flecked saliva.

"Why are you doing this?" he had cried, awakening to the horror of a blade cutting his throat. Bubbles of blood gurgling from the red mouth of his wound seemed to echo this "why" repeatedly.

His daughters had begged Medea to make him young again. But the elixir they poured down his mouth and into his wound had no magic. They cut his throat and he died. When they realized at last that Medea had duped them, they were by turns disbelieving, dismayed, angry, sickened, overwhelmed with awful grief and guilt. They flung themselves on his corpse. They cradled him in their arms. They begged him to be alive, to be old, to be sick, but to still be alive. They begged him to forgive them.

The oldest daughter (who remained inconsolable and whom the other two eventually shunned—as if guilt could be, *had to be*, contagious) reminded Medea, oddly enough, of

herself. Not that there was any physical resemblance. This girl, full-breasted, broad-hipped, and a good head shorter than Medea, was the antithesis of Medea's lean, athletic look. It was in her temperament that Medea caught glimpses of herself: in her passionate nature, in the ferocity with which she defended her opinions (however right or wrong they proved to be), in her categorically classifying both gods and men as either friends or foes.

It was this oldest daughter who, as they stole into the room of the sleeping Pelias, had expressed the most diffidence, the most revulsion, the greatest faintheartedness at what must be done. Yet, when her youngest sister took Medea's dagger and strode purposefully toward their father's bed, she rushed to snatch it from her, to be the one to cut the old man's throat, to pour the impotent drug they'd prepared into his mouth and grisly wound and, to the stricken man's dying "Why?" to murmur ardently, "Because I love you! I love you! That's why!"

What is real, what is tangible about love? Medea wondered. What is merely need, or weakness, or illusion? What acts committed in the name of love make sense in the empirical world, and what makes sense only in the soul? Truth, she thought, is a variable. There is the truth of the lover, the truth of the beloved, and the truth of the so-called impartial rest.

And if Jason should one day tire of her? If he should no longer need her? If he should cast her off?

She would destroy him, she thought. She would destroy any future he might have. She would destroy anything he might treasure. She would defile every last memory of happier times.

She loved him so.

What happens when the illusions of childhood are splintered? When things which once had dimension and solidity appear flat? What happens when they begin to crack? When darkness appears beyond the cracks? When the suspicion that monsters lurk at the periphery of one's vision is suddenly confirmed? The more fragile souls get trapped and ultimately destroyed by this discovery. But then there are the fighters who grapple with the fear, the pain, the uncertainty, the disillusionment . . .

CIRCE

CIRCE KNEW THERE HAD TO BE A TIME WHEN HER MOTHER nursed her and when, held in the charmed circle of her mother's arms, she felt warm and safe. Certainly that time existed, even if she could not remember it. Hecate, her mother, was the goddess of sorcery. She would wander the Earth invisible to all living things save dogs. Only the demonic howling stirred up at a seemingly empty night marked her presence.

The implications of being a sorceress: of dealing in magic, in the inherent mysteries of existence, in the potent curiosities, the fears and doubts that special knowledge brought

with it—this came only later. The discovery that all was
not as it appeared, that those one loved and believed to know
had alien facets to their being—this shock, indelibly fixed
on her memory, marked the decline of her innocence.

It happened like this. Hecate had a great gilded chest from
which she could, if she wished, produce wonderful things.
Circe's most precious gifts came from the chest: a purring
kitten, a flower that sparkled with dewdrops, a rainbow
that she could hold, shimmering, between her two hands.
Circe was forbidden to look in the chest. "This is mine,"
Hecate said. "Someday it will be yours, but not now."

Someday . . .

She could wait, of course; but the possibilities it presented
were so enticing. How many children had the chance to
steal a taste of a not-yet-offered delight, to behold forthcoming
joys long before the appointed time? Circe was a curious
child. So, on a day when Hecate was elsewhere, she stole into
her bedchamber and brazenly unlocked the gilded chest.

A strange perfume, as of dried flowers and moldy hay,
wafted from it. With a racing heart, she looked inside. Far
from the treasures she had expected to see, it seemed to con-
tain only disappointing bits of bark and twigs, clumps of
mud, small satchels filled with coarse gray sand, and the stiff,
brittle corpse of a bat with its wings outstretched. Had it
died in flight? Circe wondered. Had it been caught, frozen at
some high point, some exquisite moment of ascension? The
fanged mouth was wide open. Had it been about to bite its
prey or to shriek a protest against its dying? Circe pon-
dered the still form with a mixture of revulsion and fascination. This was the paradox of death, that it embodied the
ultimate horror and the ultimate peace. Truly, there was nothing terrible about a leathery lump of desiccated flesh—and
yet that very fact was exactly what she found dreadful. She
put the bat back in the chest and was wiping her hand on
her gown when she saw the gleam of the crystal.

It peeped like a jewel from beneath a handful of dry
grasses. This was more like what she had been expecting.
She plucked it up and laughed with joy at the splendid discovery. It felt cool and solid in her hand, although a sandstorm
seemed to be raging within. She was charmed by the violent
churning and swirling of blue sand: an explosion of sand

would just begin to settle when another upheaval took place. She wondered what it must feel like to be a grain of sand, tossed and flung in that storm. She loved summer storms, loved to see the lightning fleetingly etch the world in stark white, loved the bursting, rolling thunder, the pellets of rain bombarding the land.

But she had never held a crashing storm in the palm of her hand.

As she watched, the explosions subsided. The sand began to settle. A shape became visible in its midst. A demon? A god? Her mouth was suddenly dry. She huddled into herself and peered intently at the gradually emerging shape. It never occurred to her, enthralled beyond terror, to put the crystal back before she saw too much. For what would be *too much*?

The shape seemed no more substantial than a shadow. Its particulars emerged as gradually as stars in a darkening sky: eyes (were those eyes? were there were actually six of them?), details of clothing, arms, masses of flowing hair. Then came the dread jolt of recognition. It was Hecate she saw. Her mother. She identified her by the torches the woman held in each capable hand. She recognized the long fingers, the beautifully tapered nails, the jeweled bracelets, the gold death's-head ring her mother always wore. But the heads . . .

She closed her eyes to shut out the ghastly vision, to eradicate it. But it was too late. She saw her mother with three
nightmarish heads: that of a mare with a long wild mane, that
of a snarling wolf, and a head that was no more than a
white skull. In each head round eyes glowed like embers and
stared at her from the crystal.

She opened her eyes. How could it be that the mother she
knew was also this hideous creature? Furthermore, what
did it mean that this creature's blood flowed in her veins?

She was seized with the impulse to smash the crystal, to
fling it against the wall, to shatter the image inside, to
prove that it was not real, could not be found among the fragments of crystal and therefore did not exist—and therefore
was not her mother. And thereby she would eliminate the
danger of becoming like her, of growing other heads, animal heads, murderous heads with frightening powers.

"Smash it!" an insistent voice seemed to cry. "Smash it
now! At once! Before it's too late! Before the witch takes
hold of you, before she escapes, before she begins to haunt
you! Smash it! Smash it!"

And she would have smashed the shiny crystal ball, would
have flung it with all her might, would have grabbed up
the heavy candle holder from the side of her mother's bed
and broken the crystal pieces into smaller pieces and into
pebbles, and into sand.

But another voice rose alongside the first. "It's no use!"
this voice wailed. "You've seen what you've seen. You cannot
unsee it. And how would you explain the smashed crystal?
How would you explain having opened the chest you were
forbidden to touch?"

"Smash it!"

"Don't!"

"Yes!"

"No!"

What if she smashed it and the little three-headed creature emerged whole, accusatory, furious, bent on revenge?

"Yes!"

"No!"

She could not tell if the voices were in her head. She suspected they were, though they ranted on quite indepen-

dently of her. They raved. They grew louder and louder, head-splittingly loud. And then they fell suddenly silent.

It was over. The terrible three-headed woman in the crystal became a shadow again. The shadow became transparent. It dissipated like mist. The blue sand vanished. The crystal ball in Circe's hand was now quite clear. It was crystal through and through. There was nothing inside. It looked absolutely ordinary.

"Tell me about your life," Circe said to her mother. She studied her mother's familiar face, the coal-black hair, the almond eyes. There was no trace of the three beastly heads behind that smooth, fresh skin. They were there, of course. The question was, how had she concealed them so artfully? Their sheer bulk should have made telltale bulges behind those chiseled features. Had Circe not seen those unspeakable heads, she would never have guessed of their existence. What else is there I don't know of? she wondered. What other grim or surprising or dangerous secrets? She seemed to feel the tingling sensation of an alien head evolving in the recesses of her own throat. She coughed twice to dispel the feeling.

"My life is my own," Hecate answered. "If you want to be entertained, listen to the myths they tell about me."

"I don't want to hear myths," Circe said. "I want to hear what really happened. I want to know what you were like when you were my age, for example."

Hecate drew a deep breath and gazed at her daughter. The little girl could be relentless with her questions. Best to pacify her with some story or there'd be no peace. "I fell in love for the first time when I was your age," she said. "The boy was mortal. Naturally this fact precluded any happy end to the romance. My friends as well as the gods cautioned me against it. I refused to listen, however. The boy was blond with green eyes and already quite broad-shouldered for his age. He had a wonderful laugh, and we spent a great deal of time together. We ran races. We climbed mountains. We swam. We collected delicate pearly seashells. He built a marvelous castle for me out of sand.

"But he also built castles for other girls. When I found out about this, I confronted him with it. There must be some harmless explanation, I thought. I was loath to get upset before I knew for certain that there was a bona fide reason to be upset. His so-called explanation was a transparent lie. He claimed to have no idea who built those other castles or who they belonged to. Clearly they were his. They resembled the one he made for me in even the minutest detail. I was angry at his duplicity, but I felt doubly deceived by his lies. He noticed my distress. 'What's wrong?' he asked with a true face of candor. When I told him I did not care for deception, he became furious. He kicked my castle apart and trampled it flat. His violently indignant avowals of innocence reminded me of a barking dog. Therefore I changed him into a dog, a scraggly one with a short, nearly hairless bone of a tail. "Now you can bark when you're hungry and bark when you're lonely. You can bark for the rest of your life," I said.

"And did he?" Circe wanted to know.

"Did he what?"

"Did he bark for the rest of his life?"

Hecate shrugged. "Who knows," she said.

That night Circe was awakened by the howling of a wolf outside her window. Then a horse nickered purposefully. Finally she heard what sounded like an evil bray of laughter. She lay motionless, her eyes wide open, and stared into the dark. I will get up and go to the window, she thought. I'll catch her without her disguise as a mother and insist on an explanation. "How long have you had these secrets?" I'll ask. "What do they mean? How is it that you can hide them so well during the day? Do such dormant creatures exist in my body too?" Circe did not get up and go to the window, however. There was too active a possibility that the wolf would gobble her up or that the old crone would shriek enduring curses at her. What if the mare opened her mouth in what started off as a yawn but was suddenly revealed as the haunt-plagued way to the underworld?

She had to think, to plan. As much as she wanted to know her mother's secrets, too much revelation could be perilous. She was not (despite her courage and avid curiosity) sure she would not be driven mad. Nor was she certain she

would not become a gibbering waif, a pitiful, mindless little thing.

"I must take that chance," she said to herself.

It so happened that by then the howling and nickering and braying had stopped. There was no one outside her window. The moonlight illuminated a ghostly but empty patio. Nothing moved out there. Had she imagined it all? Did none of it exist?

Once she had been a part of her mother, as indivisible from Hecate as her white arms, her long legs, her fiercely beating heart. Now she felt rudely amputated from her, painfully imprisoned within her own finite flesh.

She went to Hecate's bedchamber, opened the door soundlessly, and as soundlessly crept in. The mother from whom she had been cut away lay peacefully asleep. The moonlight shone through the window and touched her face with silver. Circe stood waiting, although she knew not for what. A shiver passed through her from time to time. The thing she remembered most distinctly afterward was the gentle, almost ethereal expression on her mother's sleeping face. It was difficult to believe that behind this beloved, familiar face lurked those other faces.

One hot day a wretched, emaciated dog limped out of the woods. Circe saw it from a distance and at first mistook it for a lame wolf. It snuffled around, its nose to the earth, apparently looking for food. It did not run when she approached it, and she realized it was tame. She wondered if it was the boy her mother had once turned into a dog. The shape of his head struck her as markedly human. The small ears were rounded instead of pointed and were set low on the wedge-shaped head. This served to accentuate the high, broad forehead, so indicative of a superior intelligence. He had unusually expressive eyes, disturbing gold-flecked eyes. They seemed to draw her into their sad depths, to speak to her, to plead with her. Something undefined and mysterious linked dog and child, some common plight.

She imagined the anguish of a human sensibility imprisoned in this four-legged frame with its achingly prominent ribs. It was the insignificance of a child in a world of adults; the bondage of a dwarf in a world of giants; the extraordi-

nary torment of powerlessness that she read in this dog's eyes. She desperately wanted to reassure him that things would not always be this way. He would not be a dog to the end of his life. She would somehow restore him to human form. She would learn the secret of turning men into beasts and beasts back into men again. She was convinced that he was the boy her mother had bewitched.

The animal followed her back home. Mangy and rank-smelling as he was, she brought him around to the kitchen, gave him a bone with considerable meat yet on it, and watched him gnaw the thing clean. His teeth, she noticed, had a revolting brownish scum on them. "Good boy," she said, although she reckoned he could hardly be a boy anymore with dreadful teeth like that. Henceforth the dog followed her about like a love-struck swain.

"So you've gotten a dog," her mother said. There was neither dismay nor approval in her voice. Nor was there any sign of recognition on her face when she looked at the woeful animal. Circe had been stroking his head and observing how the gummy filth from his coarse hair was coating the palm of her hand. Her mother hated filth. Circe half expected her to insist on chasing the dog off.

Hecate knelt and examined his mangy coat for vermin. "He could use a bit of a cleaning up," she said evenly. "There's no need to cultivate an excess of wildlife around here."

The dog raised his head and looked up at her. Was it fear that glittered in his unblinking eyes?

"He seems to know you," Circe said.

Hecate disagreed. "It's only the sound of my voice that's piqued his interest." She was clever at sidetracking arguments she had no wish to pursue.

"You don't know that," Circe said stubbornly. "This old dog has been around for a while. I've thought, in fact, that there was something familiar about him; that I've seen him before. Maybe in the woods, maybe just around here. Could be he belonged to one of our hunters and for some reason strayed."

"This is a mongrel," Hecate said with a touch of disdain. "He looks like any one of a hundred mongrels—though possibly he's a bit uglier than most. It's likely you saw another dog that looked similar. This one has never been here before." No change in her facial expression belied these words.

The dog whimpered and shrank back against Circe. The girl marveled at her mother's gift for lying with such apparent sincerity. Or *was* she lying? Her smile could conceal as much as it revealed.

"I thought this might be the boy you once turned into a dog." Circe watched her mother's face intently.

Hecate laughed. "That is farfetched, though laudably imaginative, my dear."

Was this sarcasm? Was it subterfuge? She sounded genuinely amused. "Then he's not the same dog?" Circe asked.

"How could he be? That dog would be ancient if he was still alive. It all happened a long time ago, you know."

The child patted her whimpering, trembling dog and wondered if all dogs were frightened of her mother, whether or not they had once been boys. She shivered inadvertently. It was hard to imagine this kindly woman with her light-hearted laugh as the same terrifying creature that had appeared in the crystal. She could almost believe that she had been mistaken, that she had invented the nightmare mother and that her real mother, her wise and loving and just mother, was this one standing before her.

But she could not unknow what she knew. Yesterday she had awakened to a world of permanence, a world where things were what they seemed to be. Today all certainties had changed to doubts, all beliefs into skepticism. Today she understood that nothing was as it seemed and all was transitory.

"What was the spell you used to change boys into dogs?" Circe asked her mother. "What were the magic words? What did you mix into the magic potion?"

"Some day when you're older, we'll talk about it," Hecate said.

Circe nodded. Her mother had evaded the question deliberately. To realize this gave her a pang—as though calamity lurked ahead. It suggested an elemental deceptiveness in the nature of the woman she had always trusted. Hecate's broad and practiced smile opened an abyss between them.

🍎

The boy stood at the moonlit shoreline. His teeth gleamed behind his grinning lips. The waves lapped hungrily at his bare feet.

"Are you frightened?" His question, lazily uttered, sounded like a threat. He moved toward her with slow, swaggering steps. He was taller than she, and his shoulders were far broader. Did he mean to hurt her?

"What should I be frightened of?" Circe asked, standing her ground.

"Of me," he said conversationally. "I'm a stranger, after all. You don't know me."

"Why should that in itself be frightening?" She was seized with the impulse to flee. Had he seen that? Did he know?

He stopped advancing, as though to assess the extent of her panic. Yet the distance between them continued diminishing. Could the ocean waves (their rushing and lapping suddenly thunderous in the surrounding night) be washing him toward her? Though he was still some distance away, she would already feel the intensity of his need, feel the heat of his body, feel his hands on her throat.

Above them a cloud passed in front of the moon, and the boy blended with the obliterating darkness. She stared at the black space where she believed him to be, anxiously trying to locate him. The moon reappeared from behind the cloud and he materialized somewhat farther away from her again.

"I thought you were frightened because I might hurt you," the boy said, his voice maliciously casual.

"Why should you do that if you don't even know me?"

"Oh, come now, don't play innocent. It's precisely because we are strangers . . ."

Another cloud covered the moon. His words faded as he was once again enveloped in darkness. Was he real, or a product of moonlight and shadows? Had she heard him speak, or only heard the droning and washing of the sea?

He was invisible, but she sensed his approach. She sensed his hands reaching for her, sensed his body primed to thrust itself at her. "Dog," she whispered softly at her unseen enemy. "DOG!" she shouted with bloodcurdling passion. A mournful howl shattered the darkness, and, in the reeling fragments of light, she saw him—his black muzzle, his canine teeth, his alertly pointed ears, his unmistakable paw prints in the sand.

The dream had been incredibly real. It had all the earmarks of a prophecy. Circe suspected it was a message: her mother was showing her how to turn men into dogs. "So it's that easy," she said to herself. She couldn't wait to try it out, to test the degree of her power. Power was the gift that affirmed the supremacy of gods over men, of men over men, of god over god.

Supposing the dream was no more than a dream, a foolish wish, an enticing illusion?

"I can do it," she assured herself, and reviewed how she had cast the spell on the boy in the dream. She longed to be a sorceress like her mother: iron-willed, as able to change the flow of a river as the course of fate. Helplessness was intolerable to her. And being a child was intolerable to the extent that it meant being subject to the whims of others.

She took a ring from her finger and held it up to the light. "Flower . . ." she whispered anxiously, half seeing the little gold circlet change form, open, straighten, lengthen into a stem and put out a jewellike bud from which golden petals would soon unfold. "You are a flower," she intoned. But the ring remained a ring. She examined it closely, determined to see some change in it, however slight. There was none.

What had she done wrong? What indispensable step had she omitted? Perhaps the spell only worked to change boys into dogs. Suddenly the truth dawned on her. The dream had been simply a dream, nothing more.

Disgusted, she got up and went outside to look for the dog. Once agin she found him at the edge of the woods. He was playing with a baby rabbit, holding it down with one shaggy paw, letting it go, bounding after it, slapping it down, taking it in his teeth like a bitch her puppy. He's making friends with it, she thought tenderly. He's going to make a little nest for it. He's going to bring it food. She was more convinced than ever that the dog had once been a boy. It was easy to imagine him with a small furry pet, tending it, playing with it, and eventually abandoning it. Boys were all too readily bored even with the most cherished playthings.

The dog shook his head, jerking the rabbit violently back and forth. Only then did she realize he hadn't been making friends at all. He was killing it, breaking its neck. "No!" she

yelled. "Stop!" In an instant she was on him, shrieking at him, tearing at him, trembling, furious at the animal's cruelty, furious at having been duped, furious at her own naiveté, her own impotence. The dog growled and clenched his jaws savagely on the luckless rabbit. "Stop it! Stop it!" she screamed, pulling at him, striking, suddenly ready enough to murder him, knowing it was too late, knowing the rabbit was dead. The dog turned, dropping the pitiful little body. Blood foamed in his open, snarling mouth. Blood dripped from his fangs. He would have attacked her, would have leaped and sunk those bloody fangs into her neck. But all at once the ferocious growl congealed in his throat, the killer lust inexplicably drained from him. Circe gasped. Her relief was mixed with astonishment. The dog still crouched as if to leap. But he was frozen in that half-crouch and stared up past her with glazed, terrified eyes.

What had happened?

"He would have injured you," Hecate said from behind her. Of course. Circe should have known. Who else would have had such a drastic effect on the dog? Now he was whimpering again. She followed his gaze to her mother's reproving eyes. "I didn't need your help. I would have been fine," she said peevishly. A disturbing doubt tugged at her, however. *Would* she have been fine? Yes? No? Now she would never know.

"I didn't want to find out at your expense," Hecate answered, her manner detached.

It was infuriating of her to pretend such concern when she might simply have taught her daughter the necessary spells and so eliminated all danger beforehand. What caused that maddening need for secrets? "Maybe I'd have surprised you," Circe said.

"You might have." Hecate almost smiled. "I just didn't want to take the chance that you might not have."

Was she or wasn't she putting on an act? "How much do you love me?" the child was tempted to ask but did not. She knew the answer, could read it on her mother's beautiful inscrutable face: *I love you truly, but not as much as I love myself.* Circe wanted to protest, to insist that she be loved first and foremost, loved to the degree that would coutenance any sacrifice, any pain. Only then would she feel truly loved,

truly safe, truly powerful. Then she could learn all her mother's secrets, see all her faces, know all her spells. Of course that would be provoking disaster. She knew that perfectly well, although she was still a child. For one creature to love another more than itself would upset the balance of things. There would be those who were invariably loved second-best or third-best or maybe even last, but never first.

The dog crept timidly forward, still whimpering, mewling in a parody of supplication. He slunk close to the ground, more like a snake than a dog, and came to a stop at Hecate's feet. He was panting, his mouth open, his tongue lolling between his still-bloody fangs.

"Bring me the rabbit. I'll show you something interesting," Hecate said with a benign tone of parental affection. Again the question: *Was her affection assumed? Was it real? How deep did it go? Soul deep? Bone-marrow deep?* What difference did it make? the child thought suddenly. What mattered was that her mother was about to show her something wonderful, to teach her a wonderful magic spell. She picked up the limp corpse of the little rabbit and brought it to her. The rabbit was soft and still warm in her hand, and the idea occurred to her that it might yet be alive or could easily be brought to life again. After all, the threshold between life and death was precariously narrow. It could be crossed and recrossed with precious little: a kind word or a damning one; a warm arm thrown about one's shoulders; or a candle rudely snuffed out.

Hecate took the rabbit from her. "You poor thing, you had so little chance," she said. Her face wore a look of such compassion that Circe's heart surged. It surprised her to realize how much she actually loved her mother, how profoundly she could love while being unaware of that love for great stretches of time.

"Your only defense lay in flight," Hecate continued kindly to the dead rabbit. "And yet your poor legs were still too weak and small to save you ... And you," she said to the cringing dog, "your instinct is to hunt and kill. You go from one hunt to the next, one kill to the next, oblivious to the pain you inflict, and the sorrow. So I will give you a rabbit's heart that you may feel fear, a rabbit's head that you may know the helplessness of foiled escape." Thus saying, she knelt and held the dead rabbit to the dog's muzzle. He recoiled with a yelp. But as nothing further happened, he gained confidence and came closer again to sniff at the rabbit, to nuzzle it, and at last to lick at the drying blood—carefully at first, suspiciously, and then with gradually growing enthusiasm. The rabbit seemed indeed to come alive, to move, to twitch. Of course that was merely the effect of the dog's increasingly zealous ministrations. However, a curious transformation took place. The slavering mouth of the dog and the little corpse seemed to melt, to liquefy, to blend into one another: a swirl of gray hair and brown hair and foaming blood.

Circe clenched her fists. Her eyes were wide. The merging of the two creatures mesmerized her, burned like a fire in her imagination. To combine prey and predator within the same flesh was an inspiration. The fanged, blood-flecked maw shrank to an innocuous whiskered muzzle. The black nose paled to pink. The ears grew pointed and even longer. And still the animal lapped at the twitching rabbit, unaware of the metamorphosis in progress, unaware of becoming a thing that would soon be fleeing from its own appetites and

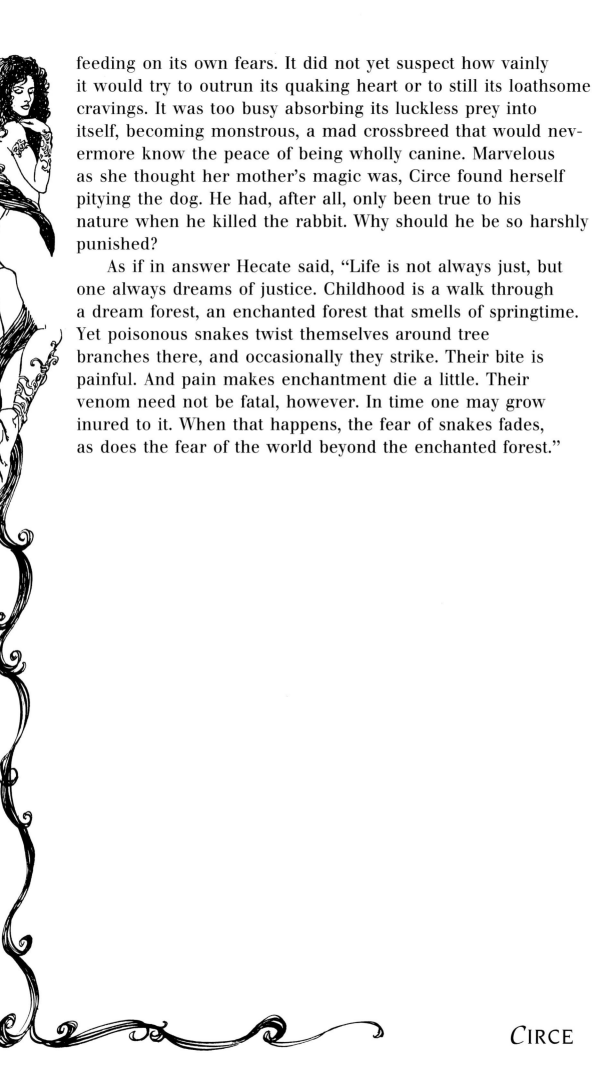

feeding on its own fears. It did not yet suspect how vainly it would try to outrun its quaking heart or to still its loathsome cravings. It was too busy absorbing its luckless prey into itself, becoming monstrous, a mad crossbreed that would nevermore know the peace of being wholly canine. Marvelous as she thought her mother's magic was, Circe found herself pitying the dog. He had, after all, only been true to his nature when he killed the rabbit. Why should he be so harshly punished?

As if in answer Hecate said, "Life is not always just, but one always dreams of justice. Childhood is a walk through a dream forest, an enchanted forest that smells of springtime. Yet poisonous snakes twist themselves around tree branches there, and occasionally they strike. Their bite is painful. And pain makes enchantment die a little. Their venom need not be fatal, however. In time one may grow inured to it. When that happens, the fear of snakes fades, as does the fear of the world beyond the enchanted forest."

Tragedies occur in which no one knows whom to blame although, clearly, the horror might have been avoided. Whether the onus here should fall on Eurydice, gentle, loving, and perhaps fatally naive (for hadn't she surrendered the burden of escape to Orpheus all too eagerly?) or whether the censure is more justly directed at Orpheus (for he had broken his vow to Pluto and me—and allowed himself the deadly luxury of falling in love with danger), who is to say? His courage should not be disparaged, nor should her steadfast love. But they are mortals, Orpheus and Eurydice. As such, they are flawed. Along with their strengths, they bear the seeds of their ruin within them.

EURYDICE

AMAZING AS IT WAS, SOME PEOPLE DID COME TO THE UNDER-world willingly. Like Eurydice, however, the majority were not given much of a choice.

"You have suffered a poisonous snake bite," the shawled and faceless shades of the dead jabbered. "Come with us willingly or we will take you by force. You have a choice."

The word "choice" was obviously a euphemism in that context. Who were these dark wraiths seeking to impress? Eurydice wondered. The shades of the dead were demons. There was no euphemism for that. So she came willingly, all the fight having left her as soon as she realized the futility of fighting. She stepped docilely into the boat that would take her across the river Styx and sat down. This will be very different from all I've known, she thought, and marveled at her curious absence of terror.

Two demons carried a woman to the boat. Her legs were crippled. Truly she appeared to be in considerable pain.

"She's one of those who agreed to come willingly," Charon, the winged and terrible boatman, whispered to Eurydice.

Tears spilled continuously down the woman's lined face and she moaned most pitifully. Who had she been? What had she been? She looked intelligent, perhaps even educated, certainly wealthy to judge by her clothes.

Charon pushed off soundlessly and without apparent effort. Thus began the ride across the glass-smooth water toward the fantastic mist-behung opposite shore.

"Why are you crying?" Eurydice asked when the relentless sobbing began to bother her. "Isn't this what you chose? Surely your legs don't hurt you now that you're dead. Isn't death a respite from earthly woes?"

"Only physical woes," the woman groaned. "Not the woes of memory."

"How is that?" Eurydice grew tense. She had comforted herself with the certainty of peace among the dead. The woman wiped at her tears and sighed with weariness. "Each thing you learn," she said listlessly, "each experience, each memory of that experience, forms changes in your brain that can never be erased. Your past remains with you always. And your pain, though it may ebb and flow and even seem to depart completely, that pain is ever with you. At least it was with me throughout these last wretched years. So I asked to come here. I asked to die, to be rid of it, to be quits with it all. But I was misled. There is no escape—at least not so expedient a one as I sought in death."

"So you think Hell is remembrance, then?" Eurydice asked.

The woman nodded.

Eurydice let her fingers trail in the water as Charon solemnly dipped the oar. Could Hell possibly be remembrance? What could this woman actually know about Hell?

She hadn't been dead long enough. She hadn't so much as seen the massive gates at the entrance.

A school of skeletal fish passed just beneath the surface, and Eurydice hurriedly drew her hand back. A stink as of mold and stale air rose from that seaweed-choked water.

"I'm so afraid," the crippled woman said. She held her hands out in front of her. "See that—I can't stop trembling!"

"Why?" Eurydice asked. "You did choose this."

"I hadn't counted on feeling so like a prisoner." The woman shuddered. "I'm not used to being so completely helpless, to having my slightest move prescribed. I have always done for myself. Even with these bad legs of mine, I have managed to get around. And now I can't. Or they won't let me. I can't decide which, but I'm terrified."

Unquestionably there were fears all mortals were prone to. But there was something worse than fear, something infinitely more dreadful: there was palpable loss.

Charon turned his gruesome head, flashed Eurydice a wry smile, and said, "They all lose what's most precious to them, those that cross the river Styx. They lose their lives, for one thing." He threw back his massive head and laughed.

Eurydice looked up at his huge eyes, his snout, his heavy jowls. She stared with such intensity that he turned away and gave his attention to rowing again.

"I've lost far more than my life," she said tonelessly. "What is life, after all? Is it a beating heart? Is it wakening? Is it sleeping and dreaming? Is it a chance to throw one's arms wide and laugh into the blue sky? Is it beholding the fragile beauty of a butterfly in flight? I could have relinquished all that with scarcely a pang. But what I have lost against my will, what has been torn from me despite my madly desperate protests, has left me sadder than sad, emptier than death, so measurelessly and irrevocably hopeless that I see no way out. Despair has replaced the fullness of hope.

"It astonishes me that I am able to speak, to sit upright in this boat, to feel something resembling compassion for this poor woman, to trail my fingers in this stinking river, to feel the weeds, the slime, tangling between them and, like a deceitful lover's touch, slip easily away.

"When I feel myself so hugely diminished that I seem no

more than an amorphous blob, when my only motion is determined by the rock and sway of this boat, when my heart outraced itself in fright, when it broke in two and bled to racking death, how is it that it can still love, still grieve, still long for Orpheus?"

The crippled woman stopped her weeping long enough to ask, "How did you die? You are so young."

Eurydice, about to answer, was suddenly at a loss for words. How *had* she died? How was it that she found herself in Charon's boat en route to Hades? Just a short while ago she was walking arm in arm with her Orpheus. There was no clear transition between then and now. She remembered how beautifully he sang to her. His bewitching songs once put the sleepless dragon to sleep. And once made the monsters Scylla and Charybdis halt their destruction just long enough for his boat to pass safely.

How indeed had she come to die? How had she lost him? How was it possible to lose someone who was as linked to you as your own heart? How did it happen that you were torn in two, you two who had been so contentedly one?

The shades had whispered about a serpent's bite. What did they know? Only what they heard, repeated interminably, and altered with each repetition—thoroughly unreliable stuff. The trouble began (and seemed somehow still to be going on) with a cosmic windstorm. Things just began blowing away. Houses blew away. Once she had fancied herself to be safe within the walls of her garden, and in the blink of an eye the walls became crisscrossed with cracks. They were blown to pieces. The pieces danced off like leaves in the wind to vanish—where else—at the vanishing point. The whole garden was blown off by this cosmic wind, just ripped up and whirled away. Only a few weeds remained rooted in what became a flat, unending desert.

"I was bitten by a snake," she murmured absently. "I died of snake bite."

Charon steered the boat ashore and moored it to a stone. Then he lifted the crippled woman out and placed her on the ground.

With a sudden fierce barking, the watchdog Cerberus bounded forth. His eyes were big as saucers, red-veined and furious in each of his three fearsome heads. Each of his

three snarling maws displayed long yellow teeth. My God, he'll kill me, Eurydice thought at once, completely forgetting that she was already dead. In any case, the animal was yanked to a halt when he came to the end of his chain.

Now the great iron doors of Hades swung open. Two hunchbacked demons with ratlike tails scurried forth bearing a pallet. This they put down next to the woman, placed her on it, and carried her off.

Eurydice hardly noticed when Charon took her arm to help her out of the boat. Her glance had fallen on an old crone, dressed all in black, who had also come through the gates. Her face was wrinkled beyond the possibility of having ever been young. At the appearance of the crone, Cerberus, who had been straining at his chain, and whose three heads had been barking savagely, grew respectfully silent.

"Come," said the crone, taking Eurydice's soft hand in her bony one.

So it was true, Eurydice realized. And still it was hard to believe she was really dead, that it was really through the gates of Hell that she was headed—she who moments before (had it actually been only moments?) had been alive, had been in love, had felt so infinitely safe in the arms of her lover, so certain of their future together.

Of course, such things did occur. Lovers were parted. Love itself died. How many grieving lovers before her had made this cold and hopeless journey? Romantic folklore promised deliverance from pain. But ultimately pain entered. The lover might swear to *belong* to his beloved, but what sort of an oath was that, really, when he could still have secrets, or long for solitude, or remember, with heartbreaking melancholy, another love that never existed?

If one could at least trust oneself never to look at a stranger with unchaste longings! But who would trust even oneself so completely? Would that the first rush of requited desire was eternal! But it changed beneath one's gaze, beneath one's caresses. What was Orpheus doing now? Was he thinking of her? Had he forgotten her? Was his heart breaking? Perhaps it was indeed only in death that love remained ageless and fresh. Was that death's solace?

They passed a canyon from which smoke billowed forth in filthy yellow clouds. A girl with brown, tousled hair and staring eyes was making her tentative way along the canyon's edge. She set each slim foot carefully on the ground, testing to see whether it would hold her weight or give way. As Eurydice watched, the ground did in fact crumble and the girl, wavering on the edge, flapped her thin arms frantically, like a bird its wings. Incredibly, she did regain her balance.

"Why does she walk so dangerously close to the edge?" Eurydice asked.

"She's blind," the crone answered. "She doesn't know how close she is."

"She's blind . . ." Eurydice repeated. She herself had been blind to the snake until it bit her. Even then, she only half understood she was dying when the deadly venom flowed through her veins. She had not wanted to understand. She'd resisted understanding. It was the fear in her that grew and grew until she was overloaded with fear and sank to the ground where she could do nothing more than await Orpheus. Orpheus would unquestionably come and, with his songs, his reassurances, his love for her, he would take all the fear and the dying away. But he did not come.

"We must help her, lead her away from that edge before she falls!" Eurydice cried.

The crone shrugged—or, rather, she hitched up her shoulders in a gesture that said, "Do whatever you want. Either way, she's already dead."

Eurydice pulled her hand from the crone's grip, calling, "Stop! Don't go any further!" The girl hesitated and turned toward Eurydice, who ran up to her, clasped both of her hands, and drew her to safer ground. She was astonished at the softness of the slender arms, the delicate beauty of the girl's sad features, her fine nose, the curve of her cheeks, her huge, unseeing, despairing eyes.

For a time they walked hand in hand behind the old crone, neither of them ready to ask the obvious questions: Who are you? How did you die? What did you leave behind? What memories did you bring?

"I remember finding lace curtains that my mother had folded and put away," Eurydice said to break the silence. "I was very little. I draped them round myself from head to toe. I imagined myself as a bride. I would have a glorious

wedding and marry the most perfect of men and our happiness would be perfect and last forever."

The blind girl seemed to smile, although tears welled up in her sightless eyes.

"What I remember," she said, "was desperately longing to be safe. Sometimes I pretended that I would be eventually. But I knew, of course, that it wasn't so. I ran away from home because my father beat me. He would smile and strike out. Sometimes he would raise his hand as if to hit me and would make love to me instead. I don't know which was worse, the beating or the lovemaking. Both seemed to rob me of something. So I escaped.

"I walked through the town, careful not to be seen by anyone who knew me. For a while I was happy. I thought: Three hours have passed and he hasn't caught me. I've survived. Then six hours passed and I hadn't been caught. But I was getting so tired. Also, I hadn't eaten in a while. I sat down on the steps of an inn to decide what to do. Men were already looking at me because I was alone and young and did not have my face covered. It wasn't long before a soldier—I think he was a soldier—invited me into the inn. I was glad at first, but that is where the real horror began.

"I don't know how many men there were. I could not keep them away. They ignored my cries. My fear and revulsion seemed to incite their cruelty. They beat me about the head and knocked me to the ground. Their hands and their bodies were suffocating. The pain and the invading darkness confused me. I became numb to their abuses. At last I lost consciousness. When I awoke, the men were gone. I only realized that after some time of feeling around and getting my bearings. My sight, you see, had not returned with my consciousness."

Eurydice could not withhold a tear, so profoundly was she moved. "But if you could not see, where did you go? What did you do?" she asked.

"I just went on," the girl said. "I was still alive and I could walk, and that was something. Though ever afterwards it happened, when some man offered me tenderness, that the dreadful event returned in flashes. I could still feel their punishing bodies on mine as truly as if they had me again."

"I am awed by your courage," Eurydice said. She had never known real physical pain except for the sharp fraction of a moment when the snake bit her and, later, the burning of the venom as it poisoned her blood. "I wish I could help you somehow. I wish I could take your pain away."

The girl smiled bitterly into the arid distance she could not see. "Can you take your own pain away?" she asked.

"My pain . . . ?" Eurydice glanced at her momentarily, somewhat at a loss. She had not mentioned her pain, had not thought about it in such explicit terms. She had been too involved with the bittersweet leave-taking of body from soul, the farewell to corporeal existence that had the unreal, enigmatic quality of a dream. Had she or had she not floated out and away from herself to be hurled across the ruined gardens like a grain of sand in a storm? Wasn't that how she found herself suddenly at the cavernous entrance to Hades? Had she really descended along that stony road studded with treacherous ruts and blind curves and precipices? Had she passed among the uncanny flitting shadows that looked like monsters, like ferocious animals, like men? And had she heard or imagined the whispered dirges, the

plaintive laments that could as well be those of a lady for her lost lover, or those of a mother for her dead child.

"My pain . . ." Eurydice repeated almost absently. The fact of the matter was that she had preferred not to think of it. As if survival lay in blanking it out, she had strolled in dreamlike insulation down to the land of the dead. For a time everything held the curious interest of someone else's tragedy. But suddenly sorrow overtook her, swamped her, stung her eyes, and filled her lungs with thick, salty grief.

"Orpheus!" she cried, for he was her greatest loss, greater even than the loss of sunlight, of rainbows, of friends, of laughter, of gathering pearly seashells and pretty stones at the seashore. To have lost her Orpheus with his bewitching songs, his embraces, his ardent kisses—this was to have suffered a mortal wound. It was to have lost a part of herself and hence to be stumbling, mutilated and bloody, through each gruesome succeeding moment. It was to have lost all that made life golden, all that raised particular moments to their exhilarating heights. It was to have lost in advance all pleasures that were yet meant for her. It was to have lost all hope and will she might yet have clung to.

The blind girl's question persisted. Could she mitigate her own pain? shrug it off like a heavy cloak? tie it into a bundle and deposit it in the sea? Could she run from it? Could she shut it out—as one shut out an unsightly view—by turning from it? Only moments ago the pain had been a phantom at the back of her mind: a loss, indisputably, but nothing to flood her eyes with tears over, nothing to tear her hair over, nothing to grow deathly pale over, nothing over which to howl in abject despair. But moments ago she had been distracted.

It was peculiar that she could become so absorbed in listening to the laments of shadows, in studying the wings and the horrifying visage of a boatman, in empathizing with the woes of another, that she could forget how her life, her whole happiness had been destroyed by one chance step, one serpent's bite.

Again she turned over the possibility that she was mistaken. How, after all, could it possibly be that everything she treasured was gone, never again to be glimpsed, caught at, resurrected, held in two hands even for a moment? It was inconceivable that among these haunted footpaths and byways there was no secret trail along which she might travel back to what she'd left. Surely there was. Surely it would be given to her to find it. Surely the gods, though known to be petulant, were not so cruel as to tear her from her Orpheus. Surely she and he were meant to be lovers, meant to be part of one another, meant to bring each other the exquisite joy of escaping the boundaries of self, the prison walls of flesh for whole enchanted instants. This wrenching misery must be undone. It must be unwound and rewound like a ball of yarn and worked into a different pattern.

"Leave me!" a raucous voice cried out. "Get away from me, you bastards!"

Eurydice had been so absorbed in her own thoughts, she had failed to notice the man seated on a stone. A vulturelike creature was pecking at him, briefly rising into the air as he swatted at it and then settling back to peck some more. Neither the blind girl nor the crone appeared to notice the wretched man.

Bearded, bareheaded, dressed in the long robes of a wizard, he sat hunched on his rock and trembled violently. His feet tapped, and his hands—when he was not making fruitless swipes at the bird-thing—beat an irregular tattoo on his thigh. Whether this quaking was caused by fright or anger or was the effect of some palsy was impossible to say.

"Why is that bird tormenting the old man?" Eurydice asked the crone. "Surely he can't have done anything bad enough to deserve such merciless abuse. Shouldn't he at least have peace now that he's dead?"

The crone shrugged. "This is how death is, my dear. Harder for some, easier for others."

"But that's not fair," Eurydice protested.

"Fairness, justice—that's for the living to banter about. Down here things are as they are."

"You mean no one is ever going to help that poor man?" Eurydice asked incredulously.

"I want to die!" the man shrieked. "Let me die!"

The crone guffawed and continued walking. "He's got his wish and little good it's done him," she said.

The blind girl shuffled slowly behind her, but Eurydice's heart ached for the wretched man. His brows were furrowed as if with the magnitude of his anguish, and his heavy-lidded eyes were almost closed. In life it must have been an intelligent, kindly face that in death was so peaked and craggy. "Let me die," he groaned aloud.

Now the bird-thing perched on his sparsely covered scalp and pecked at his forehead. The man, evidently too weakened by his exertions, did not move. Eurydice waxed indignant on his behalf. She broke a twig from a dead tree and swung energetically at the bird. It let out a shrill squawk, spread its wings as if to fly, and settled back insolently on the man's balding head.

She would have swung at it again, but the sinner (she supposed he must be a sinner of sorts to have earned such a cruel penalty) suddenly drew himself up very straight and shouted, "Get away from here, damn you!" Did he mean the bird? He was looking directly at her. It couldn't be her he was shooing off. Didn't he see she was trying to help him?

"Yes, you, stupid woman! Get away!"

Eurydice looked about to see if there wasn't someone else he meant, some other woman. The crone and the blind girl had already moved some distance off, so his rebuke could not have been directed at them.

"You want me to go?" she asked, dismayed.

"Yes, you idiot," the man spat. "Where do you think we are here, at a pleasure palace?"

"But you . . . But I only wanted . . ." Eurydice stammered.

"I know very well what you wanted—to chase this vulture away that's pecking out my eyes."

"And you don't want me to?"

"Of course not. For one thing, the damn bird's only doing what it's been told to. For another, when it plucks them out, they always grow back."

"But it hurts me to see you in such pain," Eurydice said.

The sinner's surly response was concise. "Then you're a moron. Or else your own pain is so trifling you have compassion to waste."

Eurydice was baffled. "You don't want compassion?"

"What I want and what I don't want is immaterial. Your compassion is wasted on me because I'm already dead."

Eurydice shuddered at the reminder. "If you knew you were dead, why were you asking to die?"

The man swatted feebly at the vulture (it had just pecked a chunk of flesh from above his right eye) and then slumped back into a lethargic pose. "An old habit, picked up near the end of my life." He looked unconcerned about the blood that now freely coursed down his face.

"Do you imagine you'll be sitting here with this repulsive bird forever? Don't you see an end to this misery?" Eurydice almost pleaded. "Don't you even hope for an end?"

"Ha!" the sinner snorted, wiping the back of his hand across his already closing wound to clean off the blood that was dripping into his eye. "Maybe if this wasteland were the Elysian Fields I'd have hope. But it's not. Here there is no end to misery, only constant beginnings."

"Oh, my poor man, there's always hope! Somewhere there is light, even if we cannot, in our darkness, see it."

Again the sinner began to laugh, though his laugh changed to a shouted "Damn you!" The vulture had managed to peck out his eye. He slapped the creature from his head, but his whole body trembled so violently it seemed he must fling himself from the stone on which he sat. The bird let out an astonished squawk and flapped furiously to regain its place on his bobbing, shaking head. At last it did and dug in with its claws.

"Bastard," the sinner said without conviction. "Slimy bastard." Gradually he got a measure of control over his tremors and, blinking the blood out of his injured eye, looked up at Eurydice. "Take it from one who's been dead awhile—you're deluded," he said flatly.

"No—" Eurydice began, but he interrupted.

"There's no light in the darkness. That's why it's dark. Common sense should tell you as much. And there's no happiness for us once we're dead. There's only atonement."

Eurydice, who had thus far managed to avoid thinking of herself as irretrievably dead, let out a faint gasp.

"Death, in case you have any doubt, is pain, hopelessness, weariness, and, above all, crushing boredom."

"No," Eurydice said hastily. "I won't listen to you. You must have done something dreadful to be so wretched now, to hold such dismal views."

"Cretin," the sinner snarled. "Damned foolish little imbecile!"

Eurydice turned from him and ran. In no time she caught up with the other two, who, having noticed she was not with them, had stopped to wait.

"He's mad, isn't he?" Eurydice cried breathlessly as she reached them. "That terrible bird pecking at him and that constant suffering must have driven him mad."

"If suffering could drive you mad, I'd be mad," the blind girl said.

"Now, my dear . . ." the crone took Eurydice's hand.

"Is what he said true?" she fearfully asked. "Is there no happiness ahead? Is my Orpheus truly lost to me?"

The crone solemnly nodded yes.

"I'd rather be dead than exist with such terrible knowledge," Eurydice cried.

"You are dead," the blind girl said matter-of-factly. "What do you imagine you'd be doing here if you were still alive?"

Eurydice stared speechlessly at the blind girl. Whatever she was now, it took getting used to. In the meantime it was easier to think in terms of the living: to believe there was a reason why things happened as they did; that there was a rightness to every happening. It was more agreeable to trust that though Orpheus be lost to her for the moment, he was not lost to her forever. Surely she and Orpheus, whose union had been so perfect, would be restored to one another. They would be strengthened and enriched by this heartache.

"Oh, Orpheus," she murmured, remembering her absent lover: his dark, piercing eyes, his halo of golden curls, his sensuous mouth, and his exquisite hands. When they plucked the strings of his lyre, they called forth such splendid music the birds would pause in their soaring flight. Tears glistened in her eyes and overflowed.

The old crone was uncharacteristically touched by Eurydice's grief. Though she had seen much suffering, tears in the eyes of this gentle young woman seemed quite wrong. "Your Orpheus loves you deeply," the crone said appeasingly. "So much so that he will brave Cerberus and all the wailing shades of the dead to have you back."

"How do you know?" Eurydice asked, eager to believe any explanation.

"Because it is so," the blind girl said before the crone

could answer. "I too could tell you this. Since I have lost the sight of my eyes, I can see more than before. I can see beyond mere faces and gestures. I can see your Orpheus playing his sad music for Pluto and Persephone. I can see they are stirred by the depth of his love for you. The anguish in his songs is unendurable. His grief moves them to pity. Yes, they tell him, he may have you back. Yes, he may take you back to the land of the living. Yes, you two may happily live out your lives together. There is but one condition: as he leads you up the tortuous path to the upper world, he must not turn around, regardless of the temptation. The shades of the unhappy dead will call hauntingly. They will twist and writhe in the mist. They will assume the frightening shapes of dragons and wild boars. They will play such havoc with your senses you will question which perils are real and which are hallucination."

"What satisfaction can Pluto and Persephone get from confounding us?" Eurydice asked.

"It's a test," the crone said. "They want to see the extent of your trust and how true to his word your Orpheus is."

"No one is truer than Orpheus! No one is more trustworthy!" Eurydice was indignant. "I would put my life in his hands without thinking twice."

"I'm glad to hear that," said the crone. "For that is precisely what you'll be doing."

"If it were his hand I must hold, I should have doubts," Eurydice said. "But since it is my hand he will take, I can already smell the sweet air of Earth."

Even as she finished speaking, Orpheus appeared. It was as if the sun had emerged unexpectedly from behind a cloud. Among the shades of the dead, among the mist and the gloom, his golden hair and fair skin shone like a beacon. At first she could only stare at this remarkably familiar and at the same time oddly unfamiliar man. She felt an indescribably fierce, futile longing to be part of him, to be blended with his flesh. He had come to rescue her, come here to the land of the dead while he still lived, while he was aglow with life. Stunned, she could only stare at him—this miracle of a man—afraid to believe he would not vanish if she were to fling herself into his arms. No dream could have been this precious, no wish more gloriously answered.

He took her in his arms and kissed her with all the fervor of the bereaved lover whose beloved has been miraculously restored to him. For the first time since she died she felt actually joyous. And yet there was the vague awareness of some threat to that joy, some unaccountable danger lurking. She pushed the misgivings away.

"How did you—" she began.

Taking her hands, he cut short her words. "It is through the grace of Pluto and Persephone that I was allowed to come here and bring you back," he said. "But we must go at once lest this deathly gloom corrupt us and the shades reclaim you as their own."

So they went, Orpheus holding Eurydice's hand tightly in his and leading the way. As they went, the path grew ever steeper and at times was nearly impassable. Small rocks embedded in the sandy clay constantly broke away under their feet and cascaded downward. Several times Eurydice would have fallen after them had Orpheus not been holding her hand. But he was stalwart, looking ever forward and upward. Even when she stumbled badly and yanked hard at his hand to regain her balance, he did not, in accordance with his pact, turn around. My Orpheus, she thought wistfully, I must have done something wonderful once to deserve you. Were things reversed, were it up to her to lead him through the paths of Hell, she would fail. Of this she was so sure. Her awe and her love for him swelled in her heart.

The enveloping mist thickened. It exuded a rank, murky odor that tasted like seaweed on the tongue. Now and again openings yawned in the mist like great maws—and as disconcertingly they would snap shut. The black, twisted branches of bare trees came alive in the murk. They swayed, squirmed, reached toward them. Faces became discernible in the dry bark: eyes oval and hollow with madness, mouths wide with despairing howls. It was truly hellish, this place where a tree could not be trusted to remain a tree; where the horizon line closed in around one's footsteps and even there did not hold fast but split open to reveal the hideous aspect of nothingness.

Eurydice thought: I will close my eyes and ears to these horrors. While Orpheus is holding my hand, I am safe.

BORIS ©91

This is a dream from which I will awaken whole and unharmed.

The branches thickened into stunted torsos, grew gnarled limbs, demonic heads, and still they shrilled their fiendish predictions of doom. "He will betray you!" they cried. "He will betray his oath to the gods!"

Eurydice grew weak, grew short of breath. Of course he won't, she assured herself. If I can be sure of anything either in life or in death, it is his love, his courage, his faithfulness. Thus she allayed the trembling in her legs and arms. She slowed the frantic throbbing of her heart. She subdued the awful doubts that raced round in her brain. He loves me, she thought. His love is more powerful than any demons.

Now the hellish creatures grew wings. Their hands contracted hideously into claws. Their tongues became serpents. Great, glinting horns grew from their skulls. They loomed up on either side of the lovers, a strident chorus chanting a medley of doom. The mist filled up with them. One or another of them would reach out to brush a claw through Eurydice's hair or against her cheek. Or a serpent would hiss angrily in her ear.

"This is only a dream," she continued to murmur. "I will wake up whole and alive in my lover's arms."

The claws felt like velvet when they touched her skin. But the hissing had the feel of icy kisses.

Now an indescribably loathsome beast reared up out of the mist in front of them. Its dark green hide glistened with slime, and an arrant depravity marked its hideous features. Suddenly Orpheus, who had been imperturbable, hesitated in his upward climb. The monster blocked his way.

He knew it to be no more than shadow and mist. Yet his hand tightened on Eurydice's—as if he already suspected that he would lose her, that this monster would be the instrument of her loss. But he could pass through the monster as through vapor. This he also knew. The thing that bared its fangs, that stretched its ghastly jaws wide, that emitted a screech so piercingly shrill as to resonate through their very bones, this thing slowly, purposefully spread its wings and he was mesmerized. With all he knew, all his oaths, all his hopes for their future, all his magical songs, he stood frozen, a solid petrified mass. Eurydice closed her eyes and

trusted, though she felt the chill spread through him, felt
his doubt, felt how his hands were suddenly quite moist and
cold. Still, he loved her. Though this climb was hard,
though it was terrifying, though every step was fraught with
seeming peril, he would not fail her. He could not leave
her to the darkness, to the wailing shades, to the loneliness,
to the sorrow of an eternity devoid of him when they had
come this far. He loved her too deeply. The light of the upper
world was just becoming visible, a dim, scarcely apparent
beacon of hope in the pulsing mist beyond the monster. They
were so achingly close to the top, to all they had promised
one another, to all the delights and to the infinitely precious
pleasure of belonging to each other, of loving and finding one's
love duplicated in the beloved.

Because she was so unshakably certain of his love, she
closed her eyes to the monster and to her lover's fear, to
his wavering intent, to his unexpected confusion. She did not
see the monster rise and glide toward them, though she
heard his high, sharp, lunatic chatter. "Doom!" he seemed to
be shrieking. "Doom! Doom! Doom!" And, unbelievably,
she felt her hand slip from Orpheus's grasp. It could not be
happening. Fear squeezed her heart like an iron claw. She
opened her eyes just in time to see Orpheus looking back at
her, see him staring at her in awful and helpless terror,
see the monster settle over her, the black, choking smoke that
was his body swirl round her. "Orpheus!" she cried in
frightful despair. And again, "Orpheus!" She reached out her
hands through the smoke that he might grab them, that
he might yet save her, might yet, with one grand move, sweep
her from this maelstrom of woe, might yet restore her to
the happy life they had so recently dreamed of. But he had
looked back. He had broken his oath to Pluto and Persephone. And therefore it was already too late. Though he
reached out to catch her hands, they passed right through
his, for she too was becoming mist and shadow. As she was
drawn down and down into the dark, dizzying vortex, she
called one last time, "Orpheus . . ."

A curious thing I've noted: the closer the artist comes to completing the work as it was conceived in her mind, the more elusive is the magic with which she'd hoped to imbue it. And the more torment it brings her, the more humdrum it seems. For where is the rapture, the glory she sought in its fashioning? Where is the grasp on immortality she hoped for when even this finest achievement of hers has once again fallen short, once again doomed her to a finite mortality, once again plucked from her grasp the grandeur reserved for the gods? Sometimes it is through her greatest despair that she understands, that she sees rapture flicker and beckon to her like a distant star and knows at last that it makes its brief, brilliant, vitalizing visits only when she is in the throes of creation, not afterwards. And that therefore she must keep on ...

ARACHNE

ARACHNE AWOKE FROM A WONDERFUL DREAM. IN IT THE FIGURES she had so cleverly woven into her tapestries—the mermaid, the unicorns, the monsters Scylla and Charybdis— had come alive. The unicorns pranced around her garden with high, elegant steps. The mermaid lay gracefully on a rock and sang a song of hopeless love. Scylla and Charybdis menaced the luckless sailors that passed their way, taking a morbid pleasure in the men's flailing attempts at escape from a murderous sea.

The dream had been so believable in every detail, she could hardly imagine (though good reason prompted otherwise) that the creatures she had so skillfully worked into the cloth were not in fact alive. After all, her talents were legendary. Everyone marveled at her extraordinary work. Everyone exclaimed how incredibly lifelike her creatures were, how brilliant the colors, what an astounding imagination she had, and so on. Arachne loved these compliments. The more exaggerated they were, the more she imbued the flatterer with propitious qualities. Not that her work was by any means mediocre, or that she did not deserve a good part of the adulation she received. It could literally be said she put her soul into the work. In each of her creations, a bit of her spirit was translated into portrait. This happened without any conscious effort on her part. But, unquestionably, it happened.

And if they had come alive overnight . . . ? Then that would be the end to all the irksome prattle about her being a disciple of Athena's. As if Athena had invented embroidery and weaving! As if one could not, by innate perspicacity, develop an outstanding skill.

And if they had not come alive . . . ? if it was all just dream, just delusion, just the distorted imagery of a sleeping brain? But the chance that the dream had been real beguiled her. If it is true, she thought, I shall be happy forever. I shall be modest in all subsequent expectations. I shall never again be envious.

Arachne could lie in bed no longer. She eagerly arose to inspect her tapestries. Unfortunately, they were just as she had left them. This she saw clearly as she crossed the threshold of her workroom. Yet there was an unmistakable air of mystery in the room. The echo of a song seemed to have just died away. A playful nicker might have filled the air a moment ago. Or had it been the bark of a dog? Or the rush and crash of waves?

Arachne walked up to the mermaid tapestry on her loom. It looked exactly as she remembered it, although perhaps (and this was just *perhaps*, because she couldn't be at all sure) the mermaid, with her golden curls and emerald-green

tail, was sitting just slightly more to the left of her rock than she had been. Arachne had put her directly in the center. Or had she? Memory is deceptive and colored by moods. She had experienced the elusiveness of it firsthand; had been quite positive about the details of one or another event only to have several witnesses disclaim her version. She had on occasion retired after a day of work convinced that her creation was flawed, second-rate, distinctly inferior to all else she had done. She'd awaken in the morning and find it to be exactly the reverse. The obvious question was, how could the same tapestry be a failure at sunset and a success at sunrise if not for the capriciousness of her own mind?

It was just as she was pondering this that she saw a movement out of the corner of her eye. A centaur tapestry hung on the wall to her left. She could have sworn that the centaur, a massive, thickly muscled creature modeled after Nessus, had just raised his bow and fitted an arrow into the string. She looked over. Her centaur stood just as he had been: one foreleg raised, the bow in his right hand, the right arm straight at his side, the quiver of arrows slung across his back. There were ten arrows. She counted them. None were missing.

But now it seemed she heard something behind her. And the sense of a soft, velvety muzzle next to her ear was unmistakable. One of the unicorns was about to nuzzle her ear, to rub his head gently against hers. She could feel his warm breath on her cheek and turned quickly. The unicorns, all three of them, were still in their tapestry, gamboling around a golden rose bush. They seemed not to have moved at all. Still, it was hard to think that one of them had not actually stepped from the tapestry. Arachne searched for some clue, for hoof prints leading to the edge of the tapestry, perhaps. There were none. Yet she could not believe that what she had sensed and almost seen was an illusion. These sublime creatures of hers must possess a secret life.

As an artist, she conceived and created what did not exist before or did not exist in exactly that form. She drew on the deepest yearnings of man and the secret defeats and on memories so old they were lost to the conscious mind. What is a work of art, really, but bits of the artist's dreams and agonies cleverly reinterpreted? If only the viewer

BORIS ©91

could more readily perceive the beating hearts within these
fragments—for surely they did exist, even if that existence
was too subtle for the untutored mortal eye. It must be marvelous, Arachne thought, to be immortal.

She approached her mermaid tapestry again, determined
to see something more, some sign of an actual intelligent
existence.

The lovely creature sat on a rock that jutted out over
stormy water. Foaming waves crashed against the rock
while overhead sun and black storm clouds warred in the
tumultuous sky. A boat could be seen in the distance, as
well as some specks that might have been men afloat in the
rough sea. In the foreground, floundering sailors were
headed toward the mermaid. Considering the turbulence of
the sea, they would soon be smashed against the rock.

It was ridiculous, of course, their lack of judiciousness:
throwing their lives away for a mermaid who, for connu-
bial purposes, had definite shortcomings. Such were the foibles of men, Arachne thought: blind to the pleasures within
their grasp, they squandered their lives questing after mirages. Here they forsook the comparative surety of a boat
for a salty death in pursuit of delusive love. Did that make
one iota of sense? No, it didn't. But such was the nature of
men that they would rather toss away their lives for the sake
of a shadow than live out their years under the illuminat-
ing brilliance of the sun.

"It is patently absurd," Arachne said to the mermaid.

And the mermaid, a tear escaping from either eye, agreed.
"While they were passing by in their boat, I thought I
might love them. But as soon as they jumped overboard and
began swimming toward my rock, I saw how vulgar and
ordinary they were. All the while I have been waiting here in
agonizing loneliness. I imagined that the love of at least
one, if not more, of them would bring me happiness. But
seeing how clumsy and foolish they are has crushed that
hope. Worse, I despair of ever being loved for my honesty, my
loyalty, my genuine warmth toward the other sea creatures. My father, Neptune, loves me solely because I am his
daughter, an extension of his lordly self. I doubt that he
even knows my name. I am blond, like all his daughters, and

interchangeable with any one of them as far as he's concerned. So you see why I counted on love to make me special."

Arachne was veritably surprised by this monologue. That the mermaid's woes should so closely reflect her own was remarkable. She had not, after all, striven for a self-portrait when she conceived this work. There it was, however. The psyche of the artist, it seemed, directed the artist's hand in secret.

When she thought back to her own father, a modest wool dyer, who rarely spoke to her because he would have preferred a son, she imagined with a pang how things could have been. He could have asked her what things made her laugh, for instance. He could have showed her his dyes and asked her which colors she favored. Once, when she had been suffering the aches of adolescence, she had sought him out as a confidant. "Let me tell you how I feel," she said. But he hadn't wanted to know. He had put her off—as though she might have something sinister to reveal. Did an innate rupture (contrived by the gods?) exist between fathers and their growing daughters?

Arachne was sad. She was not precisely sure why, but existence loomed so much more complex and precarious than it ever had been. She was struck by the enormity of her disgust with her father—that hard-working, taciturn, humorless man with his slavish adherence to prosaic ideology. When she showed him her work, he searched for flaws, triumphant should he find any—which was notably rare. Another of his delights was assessing its material value, although she had never asked him to do this and hardly cared. That her creatures, even her monsters, had an ineffable and quite special beauty, that the situations she portrayed bespoke life's random tragedies and rewards—all this was lost on him. "Do you find that the gods are amoral, and concerned with neither rewarding good nor chastising bad?" she once asked him. Naturally he refused to discuss it, and silenced her by curtly labeling her question "idiocy." At the time, she was bewildered. I know nothing, she thought in defeat, and was ashamed of having so stunted a view. All around her, things were happening that she apparently could only misinterpret. Since then, however, she had learned

not to trust her father, as even fathers (who were older and therefore reputedly wiser) could not be relied on for the undistorted truth.

The phenomenon of betrayal absorbed her. Part and parcel of human behavior though it seemed, within it corroded, it saddened, it destroyed. For the outrages inflicted by friends, by relatives, by lovers continued to cause suffering even when they were no longer remembered. They engendered a life of their own, these wounds that at best healed on the surface only.

It was with this theme imprinted on her thoughts that Arachne had chosen Scylla and Charybdis as subjects for a tapestry. The fate of the beautiful Scylla intrigued her. The young girl's sole and inadvertent offense was to have attracted the eye of the sea god Glaucus, who was in turn loved by Circe. This jealous enchantress vanquished her rival by transforming her into the horror that lay concealed in the straits of Messina on the Italian coast and preyed on all passing sailors. Though from the waist up she remained as astonishingly beautiful as ever, from the waist down she was transformed into six long-fanged, hideous, and rapacious dogs. They devoured all unsuspecting sailors that passed near them. Thus Scylla, so beautiful, so admired and beloved, became hugely dreaded.

There was satisfaction, no doubt, in being powerful and feared. Arachne was certain of it as she worked on the figure of Scylla. She was certain that she herself would not mind terrorizing those she considered her enemies, conceivably pursuing them as they took flight and, with the smell of their fear in her nostrils, seizing them in her jaws, letting them struggle, and then, savoring their screams of despair, biting down on them, breaking their bones, tearing them apart.

On the other hand, she did not minimize the girl's distress. It had to be unbearable to live as a grotesque, to understand that a lifetime of friendlessness, loneliness, and condemnation stretched ahead.

But it was not her ugliness that caused Scylla the greatest grief. After a time, she had gotten used to the ferocious hounds, which were, after all, a part of her. She gave them names, she stroked their heads, she tolerated their cannibalism with benign forbearance. It was the stifling sameness of her existence that she could not abide. It was the eternal lying in wait for her victims, it was the ceaseless and monotonous song of the ocean waves, it was the immutable path that the sun daily took across the sky. When she had capsized a boatload of sailors and seized the struggling men one by one, when she had shaken them until their necks snapped and they hung limply in her hounds' jaws, their anger and dread and belligerance so abruptly gone, it seemed to her that they understood she had no choice in the matter and cherished no innate wish to harm them. As far as she knew, the dead men really did understand, and continued to understand, and never ceased to understand and to console her. So she would hunker down in the water, her head just above the splash of waves, and think that it was not so unendurable after all to be a monster, to be rid of the innumerable restraints imposed by a more ordinary existence, to fear nothing and no one because they were all weaklings in comparison, to be answerable to herself only and to shape her own system of sins and virtues. Such ruminations would bring a lovely smile to her lips, and her face, beautiful as ever, would become radiant. This contentment lasted a very short time. There always came the queer inner snap—as if something irreparable had broken. Then followed the most diabolical torment: a torment beyond torment from which all respite, all hope of respite was gone. There was no woman friend to listen to her woes, no man to embrace her, however briefly. Hers was an exile from all human fellowship, from all human caring and experience.

Whenever Arachne reflected on Scylla's plight, she marveled at the parallels with her own. Her tapestries and weavings won her not only abundant praises but the slavish adoration of sycophants and lackeys, who, while they were often good for dispelling her immediate gloom, were insufficient for keeping it at bay. Each respite from melancholia was followed by intensified despair. These despairs thrust her into a kind of immobility. Her environment, her room, the world outside her room, appeared curiously two-dimensional. It appeared to recede, as if viewed from a great distance. Neither the trees nor the animals nor the people bore any relevance to her. She had become an anomaly, a dead

thing that nonetheless moved and breathed. Sorrow, as big as a clenched fist, lodged just below the breastbone. It drew all thought, all sensation thither and suffused them with woe.

Was Arachne's choice of subjects determined by her nature? She was frequently questioned on this account, and her answer was always a supercilious "I am intrigued by naked forms, not only those of humans and divinities but also those of monsters. What I aim for is always to improve my skill, to create an ever more excellent work."

There was, even so, a link between Arachne and her creations. Without question, as they took shape on her loom, a power emanated from them that drew from Arachne a hitherto unfamiliar self.

Hardly had she started to work on the figure of Charybdis when it began to exert its control over her, to dictate her moods, what she wore, even what she ate and how much she ate.

Charybdis, a daughter of Poseidon, had been turned into a monster as punishment for her gargantuan appetites. Though she had been a charming young woman, quick to laugh and to entertain her friends with droll stories, she had an unfortunate obsession with food that became ever harder to keep secret. Time and again she longed to be free of this need. But when she was not eating, she invariably thought of eating. If she sought to deny herself food, then visions of food crowded her brain: roast veal, potatoes, rich cakes. Mainly it was the vision of cakes and sweets that drove her to forsake all thoughts of abstinence. It would be better, would it not, she invariably reasoned, to eat until I am ready to burst, so I could at last stop thinking of food? While the act of eating reliably provided temporary solace, it did not lessen the angst that inevitably drove her to plan the next feast. So it was that when Hercules passed with a flock of Geyron, Charybdis, unable to control herself, stole one of the winged beasts and ate it. Hence followed the awful penalty. She was changed into a monster and was relegated to the sea, there to guzzle down great quantities of sea water along with the boats that happened to be sailing past, along with the shipmen, along with floating spars and the occasional bloated corpses of fish or men. Each time she had sucked the sea bed nearly dry, she was forced to spew the ocean back, only to swill it down again in the ensuing hours.

What happened to Arachne as the figure of Charybdis took shape is this: her hand, which moved the shuttle back and forth over the loom, took on a will of its own. It sped over the loom. It was a veritable blur of motion. Arachne had the uncanny sense of being disassociated from herself, the sense of being pointedly observed by a neutral other self that, free of the involvement of creation, commented most critically on the process. What this other self observed was the following: Isn't this woman absurd, it thought, to rush so toward the completion of her work only to feel hollow at the end? (Indeed, this was invariably the case.) Isn't it asinine that she gives short shrift to friendships, to games, to peaceful walks along the river bank, to all that might provide her some pleasure—as if pleasure were the decadent pastime of libertines and therefore to be as hotly avoided as sin?

The other self laughed mockingly, for of course Arachne's behavior was both asinine and absurd.

Isn't it grotesque, this other self went on, that despite this woman's beauty and wit and talent, she feels alive only when she's in the dead heat of creation, forgoing both food and sleep in this cause? Isn't it preposterous that she turns this effort, which might still bring her some satisfaction, into a marathon flight from darkness, from terror and from despair?

The other self, having no sympathy for overt neurosis, laughed again quite coldly.

From the beginning, Arachne had taken enormous pride and pleasure in her work. Even so, at the completion of each piece, she inevitably suffered. The sensation was akin to teetering at the edge of a depthless abyss.

Still, her work was extraordinary. Her fame spread through country after country. The nymphs of Pactolus would forsake their golden rivers to view her glorious tapestries. And the nymphs of Tmolus would abandon their vineyards with a similar fervor. But of late the distressing rumor had spread that Arachne owed her remarkable skill to the tutelage of Athena, goddess of spinners and weavers. This infuriated her. It diminished her achievement. The truth was that she had struggled in solitude, made her time-

consuming errors and discoveries on her own, taught herself to see the relationship between shapes analytically and to discern the varying effects of light and distance on color. Thus, to hear all the credit fall to Athena galled her intolerably.

"Let the miserable woman come and compete against me," Arachne would say. "I'll shame her in a hurry. I'll make her wish she'd stuck to her warring, to her swords and her shields."

Naturally, as this censure and boasting went on for a while, Athena eventually heard it. Accordingly, she disguised herself as an old, tottering woman and visited Arachne. "Hear me," she said to the young woman, "for I have been around a long time and know a bit about gods and men. Exult in your fame, enjoy your gifts, but do not detract from the skills of the goddess. Do not seek a divine glory that is not yours to have. It would be more prudent, rather, to ask Athena's forgiveness for your insults."

This pat little speech maddened Arachne all the more. She looked the old woman straight in the eye and said, "What do you know, old hag, about the discipline, the thought, the trials and errors, the torments, the ecstasies, the sheer persistence needed to create a fine work of art? What do you know of the peerless rapture, the inimitable bliss of being admired and envied by all the world? You mummified fool, can you even imagine what it must be like to step down from such a pinnacle; to begin the dispiriting, soul-crushing slide to mediocrity? Save your sermons for those anonymous mortals who have not dreamed of divine glories, who have not tasted them, who have not known what it is to excel above the finest! I won't give up my place as best, either for the sake of a witless modesty or out of the gutless fear of offending a goddess. And I won't retract a syllable of my claim. My work is by far superior to Athena's. Let her come to challenge me if she dares. Surely she doesn't need you to defend her."

"That she doesn't," the old woman said, drew off her disguise and stood revealed as Athena.

Arachne paled at this unexpected revelation. Yet even in her moment of alarm, her mind churned with ideas. The subject of love was an ever-popular one despite the anguish it inevitably brought, despite the rent illusions and formidable losses. Love was the ultimate siren, luring even the wily wayfarer to his doom with airy promises of bliss. Love, then, would be the subject of her tapestries.

Still, Arachne knew, an entrancing theme alone would not guarantee her victory. The whole conception, the composition, the colors, the workmanship, everything about this tapestry must be of surpassing excellence. This must be her finest piece. Not only that, it must be the finest piece anyone had ever woven. To do any less would mean deplorable defeat. It would mean that she was commonplace. It would mean that to have considered herself a great artist had been woeful self-deception. It would mean that all her work was mundane as sackcloth and that what she had considered the fueling force of her life was no more than a sputtering flame. In short, it would mean that her life was a joke, for which there was no more fitting testimonial than bitter laughter.

She spun her yarn. She mixed her dyes. But she sat paralyzed at her loom. She got up and paced the floor, and when she tired of that she sat down again. She stared through her window without seeing the world outside. Since this work had to surpass all others, there was nothing she could learn from, nothing she could use as inspiration or reference. How did one create such an extraordinary piece? How did one manage to begin? These problems and their daunting solutions so terrified her, she did nothing at all for several days. When it began to seem that Athena might win by sheer default, she was at last jolted into motion.

The first figures she worked into the tapestry were those of Leda and Zeus, who was disguised as a swan. Leda was demurely posed, covering her nakedness with her hands, her head tilted to one side, her bashful gaze averted from the glorious white swan so regally courting her. She had the appearance of virginal naiveté, although she knew quite well this was not a real swan but, rather, a man. She suspected that this man was also a god. There was no other explanation for the convincing guise of the swan. Which god he was, and where this union would lead, she did not ask. He loved her, this beautiful, mysterious creature. And if he didn't love her, then his courtship was extravagant and romantic

enough to pass as love. Why tarnish the dream with bleak realities? She was flattered by his ardent attentions, intrigued by his promises to make her happy, taken with the enigma of his identity and with the fantasies she spun around him—all of which were far more marvelous than how things really turned out. But the fact was that, coyly as she resisted the advances of the swan, she knew she would relent after a decent time. She hoped that by giving herself to this special creature, she too would become special. She gambled and, because the odds were not exactly in her favor (the gods, after all, being notorious philanderers) she lost.

Now Arachne worked on the figure of Danae. Danae's father, King Acrisius, had imprisoned her in a high tower to keep her from the sight of men. He had been warned that her son would eventually murder him. By guarding Danae's virtue, he sought to save himself. Arachne depicted the scene in which Zeus appeared to Danae in the guise of a shaft of sunlight. She used golden thread for the sunlight, which seemed to dance and shimmer as it took shape on the loom. The suggestion of a man hovering in its midst was so cleverly done, one moment the viewer was absolutely certain of seeing a bearded, majestic man raising one arm in an imperious command, the next moment there was no man, only an unusually brilliant column of sunbeams.

It was this oddly mesmerizing column of light that Danae saw and was inexplicably drawn to. Never had there been anything so splendid. Wonderstruck, she wanted to see it up close, to touch it if possible, to see the magical sunbeams flit and glitter in her hand, to stand under the captivating golden light, to have it wash over her, to have it kiss her eyes, her cheeks, her lips, her fingertips, her knees, her toes, to have it gently, oh-so-subtly warm her.

Of course Danae was deceived. Enchantment is no more and no less than illusion, and beauty is always too transitory. She fell in love with sparkle and warmth and gave herself guilelessly to a phantom. She saw his face only in dreams. His kisses were as fleeting as rainbows. His progeny would bring the death of her father.

The next of Arachne's scenes depicted Europa with Zeus, who had this time taken the shape of a splendid white bull with magnificent curved horns. Initially Europa was fright-

ened of the bull. But once he had won her implicit trust, he convinced her to climb on his back and forthwith abducted her.

For the bull, Arachne used the most lustrous white yarn that could be spun. The creature that took shape on her loom was truly glorious. One could well understand poor Europa's susceptibility to the beast. The bull's beauty and allure were unmistakable. The figure of Europa was fragile as a willow. Arachne used threads of the most gorgeous yet delicate hues. As Europa took shape, she appeared to embody the credulous simplicity and faith of a child. Thus were the keystones of grief and sorrow laid. Hence was Europa destined to be doubly duped—first by her dreams and then by her beloved.

Arachne drew on her own hopes and despairs to depict these tales. Her ladies were formed by the shattering deceits she had survived as well as by the radiant, intoxicating, and ultimately insubstantial dreams she had enjoyed. All who viewed this work were touched to their very souls, and many shed tears as these themes opened familiar wounds in their own hearts.

Athena, militant as she was, hardly cared to play on the sentimentality of others. She chose as her subjects scenes in which mortals had courted their own griefs by challenging the gods. All twelve Olympian gods were woven into this tapestry, Athena herself among them with her helmet, her spear, and her shield on which the terrible head of Medusa was mounted. The figures were so skillfully woven, the threads seemed to blend into actual flesh. The gods seemed to live, to breathe, to be ready at any moment to lunge from the tapestry and charge whatever mortal had been so audacious as to defy them. The colors and combinations of colors were more brilliant than anyone ever saw in real life. Their armor with its splendid detail glittered like rare jewels. The faces of both the gods and the mortals were extraordinary in their likenesses. The reds and purples of Athena's sunset skies were dazzling in their beauty. The blues of her noonday skies were achingly exquisite.

Arachne's faith began to waver when she saw Athena's work almost completed. With a sickening heart she began to doubt the superiority of her own work. Was it really more beautiful than Athena's? Was it beautiful at all? Was it not, rather, the hackneyed rendering of threadbare legends? Didn't the figures appear more like painted dolls than fated players in life's calamities? Was this truly the best work she had ever done? And if this drab, questionable production was the best, then what of all the tapestries she had woven before? Had the praise she'd received been ladled out by dullards and blind men? Had all the adulation been no more than idle puffery? Then her skill, her artistry, which had given her such delight, such purpose, were in truth mediocre. Her tapestries were indeed no better than the weavings and stitchings of any ordinary woman. She had wanted—nay, needed—to be extraordinary. Without that, without being special, her life was as devoid of color as was a cow's skull that had been bleaching in the sand for years. What she needed in order to justify her life was to be larger than herself, to be universally loved, to be a creator, to be as close to divine as any mortal could ever possibly be.

Was the work second-rate? Was it first-rate? Was it in fact a work of genius? She could not make up her mind. Her sense of judgment, her keen and infallible sense of judgment, had deserted her at the crucial point. And if the work was second-rate, if she had failed, if everyone was now laughing at her, then everything she had ever thought and done was arrantly foolish. Her deepest, most secret feelings were as common as those of a plain brown beetle making a lacy ruin of a once green leaf. What sort of life would that be: without confidence, without admirers, without a mission? If at least there were the perception of her intrinsic worth to cling to! Did anyone save the gods have that? Since the answer, as she saw it now, was no, the solution was, conceivably, to die, to pass beyond this pain, these haunting, draining uncertainties.

Arachne looked up from her loom at her rival's stern face. She saw the hauteur, the unmistakable assurance of Athena's supremacy. That, then, was the fateful judgment.

There was real and breathtaking beauty in the world. There was real pleasure, real achievement. But it could all be canceled out by the blackness of despair. Which was more genuine, the exquisite filigree of tree branches silhouetted against an ice-blue sky or the sterility of that same landscape,

so cold and bare of compassion? Which was more genuine, the attitudes and avowals of love or the indifference one could feel toward one's lover, the sense that this person has become a stranger suddenly? Which was more genuine, the passion with which one approached one's work or the gloom, the boredom, the outright apathy one could feel for it?

The answers Arachne gave herself were direct and deadly. Failure was intolerable. From that scourging reality there was but one reliable escape. Before she could doubt, before she could vacillate, before she became too frightened to act, Arachne put a noose around her neck and hanged herself.

So simple an act, and yet it might have cut off an entire future and, with it, the wealth of possibilities that time does bring. However, Athena took pity on the young woman. She had been arrogant and boastful, but these were hardly sins to be punished by death. "To create anything worthwhile always involves torment," she said to the corpse. "And even if you don't capture the elusive vision in your head, even if you fall short—as we all must—of creating the perfect work, you have to go on. That is the sacred charge of the artist: to continue always toward the unobtainable ideal."

So saying, she sprinkled a magic liquid on the dead woman's head. Immediately a transformation began to take place. Her body shrunk. Her hair fell out. Her head shriveled to not much more than a dot. She became predominantly belly and legs—a spider. And as a spider, she gained a kind of immortality. She spun and spun ever more beautiful webs. She is still spinning them, still reaching toward the vision of the perfect web that is in her mind, still falling short—though each time a little less so.

Out of the urgent need for a woman who surpassed all others in beauty, Epimetheus had one fashioned out of clay. She was modeled after the goddess Aphrodite, and while she was still inanimate clay, all who saw her were struck with amazement by her beauty. She was named Pandora, meaning "all gifted," and given wit and grace and artistic talents that should have assured her a blessedly happy life. Yet, with typical perversity, the gods also gave her a beautiful jeweled box and cautioned her never to open it. Thus she was given the haunting sense that there was danger in the world and nothing could be relied on to be as it seemed.

PANDORA

WOULD ANYONE BELIEVE HOW FRIGHTENED SHE OFTEN FELT? They would probably call it affectation. What did she have to be frightened of? they would say. She was beautiful and gifted. Her husband adored her. In short, her life was charmed. She herself had considerable difficulty in tracing the fear to anything but the shadowy and obtuse suspicion that the world itself told lies. This suspicion seemed to have developed after the uncanny experience with the seashell. She had found a lovely, delicate shell on the shore one day and picked it up. Believing she would hear the sirens singing, she held it to her ear. Instead it hooted like a screech owl, shrill and mocking.

Pandora's husband, Epimetheus, stood on the mountain-top overlooking his kingdom. He was watching a pale moon rise. She happened to be standing beside him. The twilit expanse of trees and rocks and little houses that stretched out and away clear to the ocean made her feel slightly dizzy. She held his arm to steady herself. He put his large hand over her small one like a father comforting a child. She suspected that she was not quite real to him

"You are a wish come true," he often told her.

How he saw her was unimportant to her and at the same time of crucial importance. Similarly, the persistent sense that she was not quite flesh and blood mattered and did not matter. Why did she detest the need to see herself reflected in his loving eyes? Because of the ever-present danger that he would close his eyes. Then she would be lost. For the Pandora that existed in his eyes, that Pandora, with all her power, her judgments, her talents, her flaws, her strengths, her frailties, her angers, her loves, was in truth not much more than a chimera that would vanish if there was no one to see her.

The question remained, how to guard herself against vanishing. There was no known way to struggle against it. Rather than attempt a useless struggle, she grew to accept that she had no real heart lurching forlornly against her ribs. Also, that her fears did not have the density of real fears and that they could therefore be dismissed by him with a condescending pat on the hand. She was in full complicity with him on this account. She was as unaware of her heart as she was of the finely structured metacarpal bones within that soft hand his so warmly enclosed.

Because she was nearly weightless, she could be lifted off that mountaintop by the slightest breeze. How fortunate she was to be anchored to him by the clasp of their hands.

Epimetheus gazed sternly at the ocean. Moonlight glistened on his forehead and on the bridge of his nose. With each breath the light moved and sparkled. His body blocked the moonlight from hers. Standing next to him, she was as invisible as a shadow is at night. Surely he didn't mean to

make her invisible. He didn't want her to be angry, or to be sad, or even to be envious when she looked at his intelligent, luminous face. But he didn't realize how the height and breadth of him diminished her. Or how his eyes, fixed on the breaking waves, had abandoned her. And something like anger and sadness and envy did stir in her unreal heart. On and off it was difficult to identify love among these darker feelings. Love had to be there, though. She did love him. What else could it be, this sense that she would be utterly lost without him?

And Epimetheus loved her. That was implicit in his very wish for her, for a woman like her, a wife that in every feature and gesture paralleled Aphrodite, the goddess of love. He believed it gave her pleasure when he drew her head downward along his naked torso. "This is what I love," he said. He would caress her hair gently, gently, and guide her head. There was darkness there between his legs, and a familiar terror that she always acceded to and accepted. The terror was not hers. It came from outside her, from the darkness, from the surrounding air, perhaps from him, from everywhere. It came unwelcome and unbidden, but it clung to her, held her. It made her part of itself. It imprisoned her in its bewildering reality.

He held her head, and therefore her head must belong to him—more to him than to her—at these moments. She would have liked to tell him they were both being deceived in this act of possession which appeared to involve two. In truth, it involved only one: the husband and the illusion that passed as a wife.

"I love the feel of your mouth on me," he said.

Her throat constricted. An immense pain flooded her, for there was nothing she was really giving him. There was no way a chimera could give. He let go of her head and the intolerable ache subsided. In a while she lay quietly beside him and thought: I love him for loving me. And also because without him I would not exist. And also because it is easy to love him. She propped herself up on one arm and leaned over him to see that he was watching her every move, her every breath. What does he see, she wondered, when he looks at me? Can he see into me? Can he see through me? Can he see how much I love him? Can he see how beautiful he is to me? Can he see how he is everything? Then, with her lips and her tongue—which now seemed like a kitten's tongue, small and rough and dry—she began to lick and kiss his lips, his shoulders, his chest, his arms. After a while, it seemed that it might be her own arms, her own flesh that she was kissing. They were so entangled in one another, it was hard to tell whose throat, whose arm, whose thigh, whose belly was being loved and whose was doing the loving.

"Tell me how it felt to you," he said a little later. "Tell me how you liked it," he said.

He might as well have asked her to tell him how *he* felt. Didn't he know? Shouldn't he know? "Don't ask me—tell me," she wanted to say. "It felt like a wonderful warm tickling that would turn me inside out," she said. He smiled at her, this husband did, with his dark, guarded eyes, his thick, angry brows, his sensual mouth.

"He is happy with me now," she said to herself, and this thought brought a lazy, hazy feeling akin to peace.

What she did not understand, and what frightened her, was that this wonderful cozy peace could go without warning, without any indication that it was on the ebb. She gave much thought to the fugitive quality of peace, strove to identify the warning signs, the circumstances preceding its flight. While she was doing this, he fell asleep. His sleeping self dismissed her, locked her out.

He was dreaming. She observed the movement of his eyes under the closed lids, observed the slight twitch of his fingers, as though he were reaching for something. For her, perhaps? Or for some other woman? "What were you dreaming?" she planned to ask him when he awoke, knowing in advance he would not tell her the truth. He would tell her some made-up story, something fanciful to please her.

"It makes me happy to see you laugh," he always said.

Yes, he would tell her something fanciful to make her laugh.

But the peace could evaporate quite independently of him. At sunset, for instance, when the fireflies began to glide through the twilit air. They seemed such magical little bits of life: little pinpoints of greenish fire, winking on and off as

174 ℒADIES

if to impart a mysterious coded message. What was it they were saying? Something wonderful, surely. She could watch them forever, trying to decipher their secrets. But one or another of them would invariably alight near her and she would realize, with a shock, how ordinary they were (somewhat repulsive even) in the moments when they were not aglow. One of them had once even settled on her arm and she had struck it off in horror, mistaking it for a wasp.

What was a firefly?

It was something with dimension and boundaries and mass. In short, it was something real. Something mortal. It lived and died. She could study its corpse if she wished—certainly that of the one she had struck, which lay quite still in the grass. She could pick it apart if she was so inclined, pull off its wings, open its little body to the light. But she would never find its magic, its secret. She could save the little corpse, put it in a box like a priceless jewel to keep it safe. But she knew that its substance would turn to dust and all she'd have left would be some brittle remnants: a shell, a dry relic.

A firefly was a bit of eternity? A fragment of hope?

Impossible to say which was worse, having peace or losing it. To lose it was wrenching. But to have it was to be tormented by its imminent loss. These dual concerns often plunged her into an anxious limbo in which she thought: Something terrible is about to happen. And thought: Let it happen, let it just happen, let it engulf me.

The ultimate terror was life without him. She imagined him leaving her, imagined him cutting himself off from her, truly killing her—for if she no longer existed for him, then she no longer existed. She imagined him with other women, imagined him embracing them, sucking their breasts, coupling with them, needing them for his pleasure, his happiness, as he once needed her. She imagined him making love to Aphrodite herself. She imagined each agonizing, detail: how he would kneel above her, lick and kiss her, play with her, feel her ripen to his touch. She recognized his technique, his movements, recognized his muted, barely audible sighs—as if he dared not give his rapture fuller voice lest he reveal too much. Lest he lose something like control. She recognized the odd timidity of his touch—as if his beloved were too fragile for more passionate embraces, or as if he feared to expose the enormity of his need by grasping her too fiercely. He made love as if he were afraid she would cry "Stop!"

She recognized the tension building in his face, saw the small, nervous jerks of his head, and then saw the release as, almost imperceptibly, the frown lines on his forehead smoothed out and his mouth, his warm, soft mouth, opened so slightly. She imagined him being lost to her forever, dwelled on her loss until the pain of it became unendurable. My God, she thought, is this the sort of horror that awaits me? It was inconceivable that the brain could map out a future that did not in some fashion exist.

The only recourse was to bring him back. She always brought him back. She always imagined him saying, "My Pandora, it's you I truly love. Only you. I was so terribly wrong to have left you. I was wholly deluded. I was quite quite mad."

Then she put on her most precious jewelry, looked at herself long and speculatively, and thought: This is you. You are beautiful. Or rather, she would think: This is all you are—a surface, an appearance, an illusion. Inside, you have already fallen to dust. More probably you were never more than dust to begin with and you have never become more. And finally she would think: I exist in my beauty. I am beauty. As long as I am beautiful, nothing can hurt me. This idea did not banish the threat of nonexistence, but it was a sufficient antidote, a reprieve, a sanctuary, a magic formula that allowed her to describe herself as happy for protracted periods of time. It was, after all, true that many people envied her.

There was the jeweled box, however, that Epimetheus had warned her never to open. "But why not?" she asked him. "Because it contains monsters," he said with a crooked smile. Could he be lying? she wondered. It was the crooked smile that put this thought in her head. How could there be monsters in that little box? And how terrible could they be? He's hiding something, she thought, and was frightened.

What was in the box that must be kept hidden? Was it the

secret the fireflies could not tell? Why should he want to trick her, to keep it from her? How did he decide what was right for her to know and when she would be better off left in ignorance? How did one decide which truth to reveal and which to bury? Were truths interchangeable? Were they expendable? What if she did go and open the box and glance inside? Need he know? Need he ever find out?

These thoughts seemed perfectly harmless at first, mere tickles in her consciousness. But they persisted; they took hold. What if she opened the box and there were hideous monsters inside? What if the monsters grew enormous once she opened the box? What if she could not fit them back in? What if they overwhelmed her and sank their dreadful fangs into her flesh? What if her life (which was, despite her bouts of sadness, a comfortable life, a predictable life) were to be irrevocably altered, torn open, disemboweled like the belly of a slaughtered sow? What if ugliness were to enter? What if death, grief, real loss were to enter? What if real terror were to enter—uncontrollable terror, as opposed to that terror she could control by telling herself she was beautiful, by assuring herself that her beauty kept her safe? What if nothing were to happen? What if the box were empty and nothing in the world seemed to change on the surface, but Epimetheus would look at her and know what she had done and something between them, some special bond, would be broken? What if he would no longer suffer with her pain? What if he no longer breathed a sigh of relief at her pleasure? What if he no longer laughed just to see her laugh? Can I risk it? she thought. Do I dare?

The box, with its secrets, its terrors, its treasures, lived and breathed in her mind. It unfolded there, it grew, it took on an existence quite separate from her own. I will not think of it, she told herself; she argued, she bargained: If I don't think of it now, then I can think of it later. Later it will have lost some of its power. It will be safer to think of it later. And she would sit weaving a tapestry, weaving beautiful colors into a garden scene, and think to herself: This is a good sign—I'm not thinking of it. But in that same instant of denial, her curiosity returned, renewed and terrible, stronger than ever. Her nonexistent heart began to pound suffocatingly in her ears, and then, for whole instants, would stop altogether. How was it that her husband had no need to open the box? It must be that he already knew its contents and the knowledge made him strong, made him fearless, made him a hero, made him real, made him safe, made him a god.

By degrees the certainty took hold that salvation lay in discovering what was in the box. Salvation or damnation. The two were nearly indistinguishable. Either one offered release from the consuming questions. Through this logic it came to her that she had no real choice but to open the box. Not to do so ensured that she be trapped forever in the chaos of uncertainties. The best thing to do was to give in, to give up the struggle. Do I dare? she thought shudderingly. Do I dare? But then it suddenly seemed she had to. It made more sense to surrender to her curiosity than to fight against it and be battered, trampled, flattened, decimated by it.

True, there existed the chance that in opening the box, something evil would be released to wreak unimaginable devastation. In the end, though, even that was better than this helplessness, this slow death of not knowing and of nonbeing. To embrace despair, to know it through and through, to understand it, and perhaps at last to relinquish it—was that actually possible?

"I need you, only you, no one else," he had said when she bemoaned the emptiness of adulation and the absence of friends. "The admiration of those who only envy us wears me out. I miss having people like myself to give to and get from," she had said. "I am enough for myself," he said. "As long as I have you, I don't miss anyone."

The inestimable comfort of being loved by him, absorbed by him, all her moods so carefully tended by him—what if it were to go up in blinding flame, burn, shrivel, vanish? What if even its ashes were reduced to nothing?

She intended just to lift the lid of the box a crack, just enough to peek inside and then lock it at once. It was made of rich, dark mahogany. A lovely thing, truly a work of art, with exquisite jeweled dragons carved on all sides. They had emerald scales and sapphire eyes, these marvelous beasts. Ruby flames plumed from their distended nostrils,

and their fangs were mother-of-pearl. The whole box was no larger than a baby's cradle. The lid could not possibly be very heavy.

A gold key rested in the ornate lock like an invitation. It was warm to the touch, and as she turned it she felt it throb in her hand, a living thing. Of course, that was impossible. It had to be her own pulse that she felt.

The tumbler clicked in the lock.

Would there be a dreadful reckoning? Would her senses fail her? Would the air be churned by the whiplash beating of wings? Would cherished hopes turn horrifying, like decaying corpses in ravaged tombs?

"Open it quickly," she said to herself, and grasped the edges to hoist it. The instant her hands touched the lid, it flew back.

For the first startled seconds nothing happened. Nothing emerged from the box. No cryptic secrets stood revealed. There's nothing inside, she thought, feeling thwarted. And then it began. Flames shot from the box. They crackled; they leaped nearly to the ceiling. Faces glared out at her from the blaze. Creatures thrashed about in that roiling inferno, wounds gaping from their simmering flesh. Beasts swiped at the cooler air with their paws as if to gain a purchase on it. They bellowed and yelped, drunk with a hellish agony.

Suddenly, as if with a subtle shift of the wind, she recognized these creatures. She knew them, had seen them before, and would have begun screaming herself if she hadn't, quite uncontrollably, begun to laugh. For the briefest of instants she saw Epimetheus among the unholy throng. He was calling to her. He seemed especially glad to see her. Then, before she could answer, he was swallowed up by another Epimetheus, this one with huge, snapping alligator jaws. An Epimetheus with eight thin spider legs crawled from the smoke. Another one, with the flicking forked tongue of a snake, wriggled forth. A ratlike Epimetheus, his small, glittering eyes bright and evil, leaped from the box and scampered away. Then a fifth, an eighth, a tenth Epimetheus sprang from the box until the room was filled with billowing smoke and grotesque human and animal versions of Epimetheus. Some of them were missing arms, legs, whole sections of abdomen. Some were dressed like warriors and

wielded swords. One wore a black hood and swung an executioner's ax. One was sickly, bent and old and barely supported by makeshift crutches. One floated by completely naked, his arms around a woman with flaming pubic hair. One was a furiously crying baby, toothless and chubby. A handsome and vigorous Epimetheus rode on the shoulders of an ugly, hunchbacked one. Cowards and ruffians chased one another. Lovers followed in the wake of loners. Each one, different as it was from the others, was now clearly recognizable as Epimetheus. They crawled and hobbled and leaped and galloped out through the doors and windows. A repulsively grinning Epimetheus jarred her from her paroxysm of laughter. "You witch," he growled through clenched teeth. "You've done this! You've let this evil loose!"

For a moment she saw herself in duplicate, reflected in his huge, inflamed eyes. Her hair was whipping about both of her heads as though torn by an insane wind. Her own eyes were wide and frightening. Her lips were curled back over even rows of pointed teeth. Orange flames plumed from her nostrils and ears, and a fat, wiggling tentacle (was it hers?) came forward and—

Horror seized her. What is that monstrosity? she wondered, and then thought: Is it me? Could it possibly be? But I was always beautiful in his eyes. So this shocking creature could not be . . . must not be . . . Could I have been deluded all these years? I who lived day to day thinking I was a shadow, thinking I was a mask, believing myself to be an invention of his, not a real beauty but an illusion of beauty, not happy but empty inside? Am I in truth a monster? a vampire? a beast? And if he sees me that way, what chance do I have to be otherwise?

She caught the carved wooden lid with both hands and forced it down with great effort on yet another struggling, squirming thing. Why had she opened that cursed box? If only she'd left it alone! If only it never had existed! She, who had always preferred knowledge to ignorance, wished desperately to eradicate what she knew, to make nonfacts of facts by hiding them from view, to be nothing more, nothing less than beautiful once again, and to behold him once again as a god.

Now the monsters were loping and skipping about the room. As they passed near her, she saw increasingly scary versions of herself. So he had not only found her desirable. He had found her undesirable as well. He had found her ugly, frightening, tedious. He had not only wanted to love her, he had wanted to run from her. Why hadn't he said anything? Why hadn't he told her, when she, for her part, had told him nearly everything? How do you tell your beloved she is ugly, though? How do you phrase such an unloving judgment so it will not hurt? Moreover, how do you phrase any judgment that is not true except in your eyes? Whatever she was, "ugly" did not describe it. Nor "frightening." How, then, had he come to see her thus? Was there distortion even in the vision of a god? Did even gods have flaws? Did they see these flaws reflected in others and fear them for it? This must be the explanation, though it left no chance of vindicating herself in his eyes. His tainted vision would be his tainted vision forever. She could not change that. All she could try was to somehow get rid of the monsters. To get them back into the box was impossible. But perhaps she could keep inside it whatever was still in there.

Thus she knelt on the lid to hold it down against what quickly became a frantic knocking. She turned the key in the lock. At once the multitudinous Epimetheuses scattered. The images of her monstrous selves vanished. The smoke cleared. But who am I? she wondered. Her question was lost

182 *LADIES*

in the barrage of knocking from inside the box. As she listened to the feverish pounding of the captured thing, she imagined what it was still yammering inside there. It might indeed be the thing that could bring salvation—the one thing that was not freakish or terrifying or sad: hope.

Yes, when Epimetheus had seemed so distant, when he had seemed so estranged from her, or when she had seemed so insignificant to herself, she never had stopped hoping that things would change. When she was sad, she'd abidingly clung to the hope that things were not as they appeared—or if they were, that they would not always be so. She hoped one day to penetrate his guises, his performances, his masks. She hoped to embrace him wholly and truly. She hoped that he might see beyond her beauty, see her fears, her flaws, her secrets, her dreams and love her nonetheless.

As though the wooden box were transparent, she could see the struggling captive inside, see its lucent wings vainly beating the air, see its silky chest rise and fall with exasperated breath, see its small body grow luminous with its frantic effort.

How desperately she wished she could reverse time and direct the henceforth unfolding events more cleverly. But if she had power over the flow of time, how would she in fact use it? Would she play the docile, hollow lady she'd played before? Would she get entangled in the same woes? Then she'd end up kneeling at the same carved box, her hands pressed desperately down on the same lid, her ears filled with the same frantic hammering of hope.

One can pass all one's days in relative innocence. One can grow horns and cloven hooves and scarcely notice it. One's lover can by sly means indicate that he has mislaid his heart. One offers a vague purr of sympathy and forgets it at once. But the missing heart beats, the hooves trample, the horns inadvertently hook into flesh. Murders have occurred for which no one had an explanation. The mystery unravels beneath its surface.

Since Pandora had seen her beloved Epimetheus as an old man, a young man, a coward, a fool, a monster, a hero, a scoundrel, a torturer, a martyr; since she had seen herself as a Harpy, a giantess, a poisonous beast, indestructible as

stone, fragile as a flower, she could not go back to Epimetheus on the pretext that they could live the life they'd lived before or dream the dreams they'd dreamed. Never again could she look at this god she'd known without seeing the holes in his flesh, the putrescent wounds, the demonic shapes. Never again would she think herself nothing more than a lovely shell, an insubstantial shadow, directionless as a leaf at the mercy of winds. Within the shell there were sharp claws, there were flashing eyes, there were strengths, passions, rages, depths unplumbed.

"What did we really have?" she cried to her absent husband. "Was it all just a fantasy? Was it frail, beautiful as a rainbow, and, as a rainbow, transient? Was it no more than sunlight dancing on water and then vanishing as if it had never been? If the god I worshiped with all my heart is so truly flawed, then I was obscenely deluded in my adoration. The pity of it is that had you showed me the gruesome wounds in your flesh, had you showed me your savage and monstrous faces, I would have loved you anyway.

"Once I blessed the day I first loved you. Now I curse it. Once I believed it to be an enchanted beginning. Now I see it, rather, as the beginning of my world's end. I loved you unreservedly. I accepted our differences—those pieces so impossible to fit together—as the glue that fused us to each other. I wanted nothing more in life than to make you happy. You created me and I remained malleable, knowing how it pleased you to shape me. I loved you lazily, acquiescently, so that you could be the undisputed lord.

"I was so wholly yours, I never dreamed how terribly you could deceive me. And what now? How can I go on living, day after day, knowing what I know? Will it not, rather, be dying that I do bit by bit daily? Will I not, rather, be tearing my clothes, pounding my fists against the pillows until I collapse, exhausted to death? Will I not lie there remembering how once no love seemed more perfect than ours and how this perfect love was destroyed by secrets and deceptions and lies?

"I never dreamed that I could loathe you so, you who once were my life, my very soul. But in deceiving me, you murdered my love. For that, no curse is vile enough to sate my rancorous heart. Nor would mere torment throughout eternity suffice. I hope that your wounds take indecently long to heal. I hope they reopen whenever you forget them. I hope your healing will be an ageless process, painful and humbling. I hope you will know the emptiness of spurious posturing. I hope your blood runs black in your veins and fetid as swamp water.

"Once I loved you wholly as ever any babe its nurse, accepting all her smiles, her milk, the cradling in her arms as love and asking naught but that this loving endure forever. I loved you purely as the pious do their gods, wishing only to charm you, to adore you, to give you whatever it was that would bring you pleasure. Now I wish you wretchedness, agony, and despair. I wish you to know the world as frightful, the days as blazing and crowded with enemies, the nights as rent with unspeakable shocks and black as a pit full of poisonous vipers.

"And yet (how this takes me by surprise!) my rancor abates in sea-salt gusts of wind when I hear hope stir and move inside this box. I begin to imagine that between the injuries and the losses we might dredge up enough words to say, 'You matter to me'—precarious words haunting the dark circles around our eyes. I begin to imagine that the smoldering white days and demonic black nights might lend us cause to reach for each other's hands. I imagine that by the light of a burned-out afternoon, we might get an unvarnished look at one another and find the hope to begin anew."